OTTO
TATTERCOAT and the
FOREST of LOST THINGS

Also by Matilda Woods

The Boy, the Bird & the Coffin Maker
The Girl Who Sailed the Stars

OTTO
TATTERCOAT and the
FOREST of LOST THINGS

MATILDA WOODS

PHILOMEL BOOKS

PHILOMEL BOOKS
An imprint of Penguin Random House LLC, New York

First published in the United States of America by Philomel, an imprint of
Penguin Random House LLC, 2020.

Text copyright © 2020 by Matilda Woods.
Illustrations copyright © 2020 by Kathrin Honesta.

First published in Great Britain by Scholastic Ltd in 2020.

Philomel Books is a registered trademark of Penguin Random House LLC.

Visit us online at penguinrandomhouse.com

LIBRARY OF CONGRESS CATALOGING-IN-PUBLICATION DATA
Names: Woods, Matilda, author.
Title: Otto Tattercoat and the forest of lost things / Matilda Woods.
Description: New York : Philomel Books, 2020. | Audience: Ages 8-12.
| Audience: Grades 4-6. | Summary: Left alone in Hodeldorf, the coldest
city anywhere, Otto joins forces with Nim and other tattercoats, street
children who steal to survive, to face evil forces and save the day.
Identifiers: LCCN 2020012700 (print) | LCCN 2020012701 (ebook)
| ISBN 9780525515272 (hardcover) | ISBN 9780525515289 (epub)
Subjects: CYAC: Street children—Fiction. | Homeless persons—Fiction.
| Robbers and outlaws—Fiction. | Missing persons—Fiction. | Fantasy.
Classification: LCC PZ7.1.W663 Ott 2020 (print) | LCC PZ7.1.W663 (ebook)
| DDC [Fic]—dc23
LC record available at https://lccn.loc.gov/2020012700
LC ebook record available at https://lccn.loc.gov/2020012701

Printed in the United States of America

ISBN 9780525515272

1 3 5 7 9 10 8 6 4 2

Edited by Liza Kaplan.
Design by Ellice M. Lee.
Text set in Goudy Old Style MT.

For Hector
2008–2018

OTTO TATTERCOAT and the FOREST of LOST THINGS

+ · Chapter One ·+·

THE COLDSTORM

The people of Hodeldorf knew it was a coldstorm long before the three bells tolled. The signs were all around: the wind howled like it was in pain, the hands on the clock tower snapped, and when you tried to breathe you coughed the air back out. It was so icy the feathers of birds froze as they flew, and the birds fell like stones out of the sky. It was one such bird—a rather large tree sparrow—that woke the storekeeper up.

"Blasted tattercoats!" the storekeeper grumbled to his wife when he heard the thump on their roof. "If I had a nickel for each time one of those children slept beside our chimney, I'd be rich."

"You already are rich," his wife pointed out.

"Well, I'd be even richer." The storekeeper threw off his blanket and got out of bed.

"Leave it tonight," his wife said. "You heard the bells. It's a coldstorm. It's not safe to go outside."

"You know what isn't safe? Dirty children scurrying about on *our* roof. If we don't shoo them away, they'll gather like a pack of wolves and fall right through the ceiling. We'll be squashed in our beds!" He hated all children, but filthy little tattercoats who stole from his store and slept on the roof were the worst type of children of all.

The storekeeper put on three coats, grabbed a fire iron, and headed outside. A blast of frozen air greeted him, but his anger fueled him and kept him warm.

"Get off!" he yelled into the sky. "Get off my roof, or I'll call the guards!"

The only response was silence. The storekeeper crossed the road and looked up at his roof. Instead of seeing a tattercoat huddled beside his chimney, he saw a frozen bird.

"Blasted sparrows," the storekeeper mumbled. He was about to go back inside when he saw two people huddled against the wall of his house. That was hardly better than finding them on his roof.

"Up you get! Be on your way!" he yelled.

The man and woman didn't move. Their coats were wrapped tightly around them so that only the top halves of their heads stuck out. A thin dusting of snow lay upon their heads. More snowflakes drifted down from the icy sky. The pair appeared to be asleep.

"Shoo," the storekeeper said as he poked them with the sharp end of the fire iron. They still didn't move.

"Wolves and witches and never-ending woods," the storekeeper cursed. They were dead.

Unable to do anything about them tonight, the storekeeper turned to go back inside. Then he heard a small cry. The man and woman remained motionless, but something moved beneath their coats.

Reluctantly, the storekeeper pulled aside the cloth. A young girl lay underneath, nestled between her parents. The cold that had claimed them had yet to claim her.

The storekeeper wondered what to do. If he left the child out here, she would die. If he brought her inside, his wife would want to keep her.

"I can't have that," he said. "Better get rid of you before she sees." Though he didn't care for children, he also didn't care for them freezing in the streets. In a place like Hodeldorf, that happened a lot.

The girl cried as the storekeeper pulled her from her parents' icy grasp. Her coat was very thin and did barely anything to keep her warm. He carried her off into the night.

"I know just the right place for you," he said.

In Hodeldorf, there was only one place to take lost children: Frau Ferber's Boot Polish Factory.

The storekeeper trudged through the empty streets of the city, leaving a trail of footprints in the snow. He reached a small dark door and knocked sharply. A woman answered. She was dressed in black and wore her hair tied in a bun. It was Frau Ferber.

"Sorry to disturb you," the storekeeper said. "But I thought you might be able to help."

"You're too poor to care for your child?" she guessed.

"I'm not poor, and she's not my child," the storekeeper snapped. "And I didn't snatch her either," he was quick to add. "Her parents died in the coldstorm, and I can't look after her."

Frau Ferber looked at the girl nestled against the man's chest and frowned. "She's a bit small to work in the factory."

"Please, Frau Ferber," the man said. The girl, having fallen asleep, was unaware of the conversation taking place about her. "She has nowhere else to go."

"Show me her hands."

The storekeeper held up one of the girl's hands. She stirred slightly. Her hand was very small and pale.

"They *would* fit very nicely," Frau Ferber remarked.

"What do you mean?" the man asked.

"I mean that I will take her," Frau Ferber said. "Does she have a name?"

The man was about to say he didn't know her name when he saw something written on the collar of her coat.

"Elke," he said, before handing the girl over.

"Don't worry, Elke." Frau Ferber carried the girl inside. "I'll look after you now."

The factory door closed. The storekeeper heard a key turn in the lock. The sound made his heart skip a beat. Even though he had saved the little girl from the cold, he couldn't shake the feeling he had put her in danger of something else. There was something about Frau Ferber he didn't like: something about the way she had looked at the child when she carried her inside. Frau Ferber had looked at the girl the same way he looked at money or a fine set of jewels. There was no love in that gaze, only greed. Why would someone look at a child like that?

Chapter Two

THE COLDEST CITY IN THE WORLD

....

Ten Years Later

Otto peered out the window of the train at trees that rose like giants into the sky. Thick snow made their branches hang low. Among the dark shadows, Otto saw movement. Creatures were slinking about in the darkness, watching them pass. He was sure of it. Otto shivered. It felt like whatever was in the woods was watching him now. He shuffled closer to his mother.

"We're almost there," his mother said with a smile. She hadn't noticed anything odd about the trees. "The city's just beyond the woods."

The trees cleared, and the city of Hodeldorf came

into sight, surrounded by a large stone wall. The icy wind had peeled all the paint from the walls, so every building in the city was the same dull gray. Snow lay thick upon the roofs, and smoke chugged out from thousands of little chimneys as the fires in the homes below desperately fought to keep the cold out. The train pulled into the station. It was gray too. Otto and his mother were the only two passengers to disembark.

Hodeldorf greeted them with the coldest blast of air they had ever felt. Snow lay heavy upon the platform. No one had made attempts to clear it. The platform was deserted. For a moment, it felt like they were the only two people in the world. Then they caught sight of the stationmaster.

The stationmaster sat in a small office. When he didn't come to greet them, they trudged over to greet him. Otto's mother knocked on the office window, and the stationmaster jumped and looked up. He put on one coat and then another before stepping outside.

A wave of heat escaped the office, but the icy air gobbled it up in an instant.

"Hello," Otto's mother said. The cold air pinched her cheeks and made them red. "I was wondering if—"

"The next train leaves in two hours," the stationmaster said, cutting her off. The quicker the conversation ended, the quicker he could get back to the warmth of his office.

"Why are you telling me that?" Otto's mother asked.

"So you don't miss it."

"I don't care if we miss it. We don't want to leave, on account of only just having arrived."

The stationmaster looked confused. "Are you sure?"

"Of course I'm sure," Otto's mother snapped. "We just got off that train." She pointed to the green-and-gold train, which was now being loaded with crates of black jars.

"Well, best get back on it," the stationmaster said.

"Whyever would we do that?"

"Because no one comes here. Not anymore. Hodeldorf is the coldest city in the world."

"That's exactly why we've come," Otto's mother said. "Now, where's the nearest inn?"

"He was right, you know," Herr Kruger told Otto and his mother as they climbed the stairs of his inn. "Hodeldorf's been getting colder for over fifty years. It's cold in winter, it's cold in spring, it's even cold in summer. I can't remember the last warm day, and I turn fifty next year."

"It was cold in Dortzig too," Otto's mother pointed out.

"Not like the cold here," Herr Kruger warned.

They stepped onto the landing, and Herr Kruger led them to a room on their right.

"Now, it's one silver a night. That includes two hot breakfasts. The dining room is downstairs, and the bathroom is at the end of the hall. Wood for your fire is delivered every evening, and if you hear the clock tower toll three times, make sure you don't let the fire go out."

"Why not?" Otto asked.

"Because three tolls mean there's a coldstorm coming. If you let the fire go out, you'll freeze to death in your sleep."

Great, Otto thought to himself. He'd never wanted to come to Hodeldorf in the first place. It had been his mother's idea. Now he had his first reason to leave. Who wanted to live in a place so cold you could freeze in your sleep?

Herr Kruger unlocked their room and left them to settle in.

"My, doesn't this feel cozy?" Otto's mother said as she looked around the room. It was a very quick look, for it was a very little room. "Once I've sold a few coats, we'll be able to move into our own place, just like we had in Dortzig."

"About Dortzig," Otto said. "I wish we hadn't left." Things had been good there. It hadn't exactly been warm, but it had been warmer than this place, and he'd had friends, and his mother had owned her own shop. It had had gold-trimmed glass windows that looked out over the main square. She had been the best seamstress in Dortzig.

"I know you're sad, but this will be an adventure. Didn't you feel cramped in Dortzig, Otto? All squished in?"

"I feel more squished in here," Otto said, looking mournfully around the room. "How many coats do you have to sell before we can get a house?"

"Oh, three or four or five or ten." His mother waved her arm absently in the air. When she saw her son's face pale, she put down her bags and knelt in front of him. "Don't you worry, Otto. When our first store burned down in Dortzig, you thought it was the end of the world. But then I bought another that was even grander. Remember all that gold trim?"

Otto nodded.

"And when your father fell sick and passed away, you cried for weeks and weeks. I couldn't bring him back, but do you remember how I made you feel better?"

"You loved me twice as much."

"That's right. And now we've moved to the coldest place in the world, but we're going to be fine."

"How do you know?"

"Because we came here together. And as long as we're together, we're going to be okay."

"Promise?" Otto said.

"Promise." His mother wrapped him in a warm hug, and for the first time since he stepped off the train, Otto forgot all about the cold. "Now, off you go to bed. I'll stack the fire tonight and head out first thing in the morning to start selling my coats. I'll be back before midday, and we can have lunch together."

The following morning, Otto woke to the sound of Herr Kruger delivering his breakfast.

"Your mother asked me to bring it up so you could eat in bed." Herr Kruger placed the tray in front of Otto. There was warm toast, marmalade, and two boiled eggs. "She ate before dawn and was out at first light."

Otto thanked Herr Kruger for the food, and the innkeeper left.

Otto ate his meal and then stood by the window, looking down over the dull city. He searched among the people bustling below, on the lookout for a bright red coat—that was what his mother wore. But he couldn't spot her. She must have ventured farther away.

Otto sat by the fire for a little while and then went back to bed. When he awoke, the sun was setting. He looked around the room. His mother wasn't there, and the fire was almost out.

Otto put some logs in the fire and stood by the window, looking down over the city. As night fell, the crowds dispersed. Not a single person wore a coat as red as his mother's.

A boy delivered more wood for the night.

"Excuse me," Otto said as the boy stacked the wood in the corner. "Have you seen my mother anywhere?"

The boy shook his head and hurried off to deliver wood to the next room.

Down below, the streetlamps were being lit. By the flickering light, Otto continued to search for his mother. When his legs grew tired, he pulled a chair over to the glass and rested his head against the icy pane. The clock tower tolled one hour and then two and then three. Otto's eyes drifted closed, and he fell asleep.

When Otto awoke, weak sunlight trickled through the window. He looked over to his mother's bed. It remained untouched. The fire had almost gone out. Something was wrong: his mother had never left him alone for this long. He would have to go outside and find her.

Chapter Three

"YOU CAN'T TRUST ANYONE"

"**C**abbages and moldy bread!" Otto cursed as he was hit by another blast of wind. It passed right through his coat like he wasn't even wearing one. Out of all the places his mother could have gone missing, why did it have to be Hodeldorf?

The streets of the city were as dull and bleak as Otto's thoughts. He'd been searching for his mother for over a week and was still no closer to finding her. Everyone he asked had no idea where she was. It was like the wind itself had carried her away.

Otto had just turned onto a smaller street near the main square when a girl appeared beside him.

"That sure is a fine coat," the girl said. She looked a little older than Otto. She had wild brown hair, almost as wild as the woods surrounding the city, and skin as pale as the snow. "Who'd you steal it from?"

"I didn't steal it from anyone," Otto replied. "It's my coat, given to me true and proper."

"By who?"

The girl walked around Otto in a circle, admiring the coat from every angle. Otto, however, didn't admire *her* coat. It was sad and gray with at least five holes in the right sleeve alone. If anyone in the city needed a coat made by his mother, it was her. She must have been freezing.

"I'm not telling," Otto said. He folded his arms across his chest and stepped away from the girl in the tatty coat.

"Ha!" the girl said. "If you won't tell me who gave it to you, that means you stole it."

"No, I didn't!" he protested. "My mother gave it to me. She made it. Have you seen her?"

"I'm not sure. I don't know what she looks like."

"She's about this tall." Otto raised his arm as high as it would go. "And as thin as you. She has brown hair like me and brown eyes to match. So, have you seen her?"

The girl thought for a moment and then shook her head. "I don't really notice what people look like. What coat was she wearing? Did it look like yours?"

"No. Her coat is red with a white fur trim."

"Sorry. I've never seen a coat like that." The girl

sounded certain, and in fact, if anyone in the city would have noticed that coat, it would have been her. She estimated that at least one-quarter of all her thoughts were about coats, and at least half of those thoughts were about the coat she currently wore. She had stolen the coat when she was eight. It had been bright yellow back then; that's what had caught her eye. Now, four years later, it had faded to a sad gray, and the cloth was so thin it barely kept any warmth in.

Next time she would steal a thicker coat, perhaps something lined with wolf or fox fur. But she couldn't steal one yet; that was against the rules. She had to wait until her current coat was so worn it was threadbare. Only then would she be allowed to discard it and choose a new one.

"Oh." Otto's body slumped with disappointment.

"What color would you call that?" the girl asked.

"Huh?" Otto said.

"Your coat," she clarified. "What color would you call your coat?"

"Green, I guess." Otto didn't care about the color of his coat. He had more important things to worry about.

"I can see it's green," the girl continued. "But what type of green?"

"Emerald, I suppose. That's what my mother called it: my emerald-green coat."

"And what's it made of? It looks soft."

"I'm not sure," Otto said.

"Can I touch it?" Before Otto could say no, the girl ran her fingers along the emerald sleeves and over the thick pockets. Eventually, she let go of the coat and looked up at the boy. "What's your name?"

"Otto."

"I'm Nim." She shook his hand. "Is your coat new?"

Otto shook his head. "I've had it for a year."

"I've never seen it before. Are you new to Hodeldorf?"

"I'm from Dortzig. My mother wanted to come here. She's a coat maker. But business in Dortzig isn't what it used to be, and she thought lots of people would want coats in Hodeldorf. She could probably make you another one if I ever find her."

Nim looked extremely offended by this. "No self-respecting tattercoat would wear two coats," she said. Then, after a pause, she remarked, "I've never met a coat maker before. Your mother must be real good. That's the finest coat I've ever seen."

"She's the best at making coats," Otto agreed.

Nim wished she had a mother, even just a lost mother who couldn't make coats at all. But she knew it wasn't to be. She was a tattercoat. That meant she had to sleep on the rooftops and look after herself.

Nim was about to ask another question about the

coat when a black-haired boy raced down the street. He grabbed the right sleeve of Otto's coat and began to pull it off.

"Hey!" Otto yelled. He tried to push the boy away. "This is mine!"

"Not anymore," the black-haired boy said. He scuffled with Otto for several seconds. Eventually, he pulled one sleeve off and then the other. The coat fell into his hands. He shoved it under his arm and ran into the crowd.

"Hey," Otto screamed. "Give it back!" He turned to give chase, but tripped over in the snow, and when he looked up, the boy was nowhere to be seen. "Thief! Thief!" Otto called helplessly, but no one in the crowd turned to look except for Nim.

"No one turns when they hear that word," Nim said. Otto looked far less grand without his emerald coat. "We're all thieves down here. Even the animals. Take Nibbles, for instance." Nim reached into her right pocket and pulled out a scraggly old gray rat. He had wonky whiskers from getting trodden on, and quite a few were missing. He was wearing a tiny faded blue coat of his own. "He's the second-best thief I've ever met."

"That's a rat!" Otto said, stepping away. He wrapped his arms around his chest. Partly, it was to get away from the rat, but mainly it was to keep out the cold.

"Sure is," Nim said proudly. "Isn't he grand?" She stroked the rat lovingly with her finger.

Otto looked disgusted.

"The only thief better than Nibbles is Blink," Nim said. "He's the one who just stole your coat."

"Where'd he go?" Otto asked. Without a coat to protect him, Otto had begun to shiver. His hands were turning purple. He put them in his pant pockets to keep his fingers warm.

"No one knows. Blink just appears from time to time, grabs something he wants—usually a coat—and then disappears. Once, no one saw him for a month. All us tattercoats thought he was dead until he stole five schnitzels in the main square."

Otto was about to ask what tattercoats were, when he realized he had been robbed of something else. His pant pockets were empty.

"Hey," he said. "Someone stole my money." He was about to blame Blink when he noticed the rat in Nim's hand was chewing on something silver.

"Where'd you get that coin?" Otto said.

"Er . . ." Nim shoved Nibbles back into her pocket. "What coin?"

"You're a thief too!" Otto yelled. He looked at Nim and then at her wriggling pocket. Nibbles had stuck his head out again and was waving the silver coin triumphantly above his head. "You're both thieves!"

"Well, you can't say I didn't warn you," Nim said. "We're all thieves down here."

Otto shook his head. "You're just as bad as Blink."

A cloud of anger crossed Nim's face. Even Nibbles looked offended by that comment.

"How dare you?" she said. "I'm not at all like Blink. I was going to give you back your coins. But after that accusation, maybe I'll keep them for myself."

"Then you really will be as bad as him," Otto said. His lower lip began to tremble. Not only had he lost his mother and his coat, but now he had lost all his money. What was he going to do?

Nim looked like she wanted to disappear into the crowd. But instead she took the coin from Nibbles and pulled five more from her pocket. She handed them back to Otto.

"I'm sorry," she said.

Otto was about to thank her when he realized one coin remained missing.

"Where is it? The last coin?"

"In my pocket."

"Give it back." Otto held out his hand. "It's mine."

"But I earned it," Nim said.

"Earned it? What are you talking about?"

"It's payment for our service," Nim said. "If me and Nibbles hadn't stolen the coins, Blink would have taken them all, and you never would have gotten any of them back. Thanks to me and Nibbles, you'll be able to buy your dinner."

On that note, Nim decided it was time for her and Nibbles to leave.

"Goodbye, Otto," she said to the boy without a coat. "I hope you find your mother. And be careful. You can't trust anyone 'round here."

Otto wondered whether she was right.

Chapter Four

THE BLACK-HANDED GIRL

"A in't it beautiful, Nibbles?" Nim said as she held the silver coin up under the dim winter sun.

Nibbles poked his head out of her pocket and twitched his whiskers in the cold air. It was like he could smell their good fortune—like he could smell there was a very fine feast coming their way.

"And right you are," Nim said as they headed toward the main square. "But not a very large feast," she warned. "If we eat too much, we'll spew it all back up, and then it would be wasted."

The crowd grew larger as they approached Hodeldorf Square. Nibbles scampered onto Nim's shoulder, where he had a fine vantage point for all the treats up ahead.

Nim and Nibbles smelled the chicken frying in Herr Muller's schnitzel store, the batter bubbling away in Frau Neumann's pancake house, and the thick, juicy pork hocks stewing away in Herr Kruger's Inn. After inspecting every food stall, they decided to buy something sweet and warm.

The store bell twinkled as Nibbles and Nim stepped inside. The shop was warm and bright, and Nim felt her cheeks grew rosy with color.

"Look, Nibbles," Nim whispered as she inspected the pastries steaming up the glass cabinets around her. "Look at all that jam oozing out. And I've never seen such a rich-looking custard."

Nim approached the counter and smiled up at the storekeeper. The man's own smile dropped when his eyes fell upon Nim.

"Get out," the storekeeper said. "Get out of my store. I'll have none of your sort in here. It's bad enough half of you sleep on my roof. Even when I spray you lot with water, you never leave. Now shoo!" He waved his arms toward the door. "You're thieves. The whole lot of you. Get out."

"But I'm here to buy my supper, not steal it," Nim said. "See?" She reached into her pocket and pulled out her silver coin.

"And how did you get that?" the storekeeper asked. "Stole it, I suppose?"

Nim shook her head. "I was given it by a gentleman for providing him a service."

The storekeeper looked very skeptical about this. So skeptical, in fact, that he grabbed a broom from the corner of the store and tried to brush Nim out the door. Unfortunately for him, Nim was not a speck of dust that lay motionless on the floor. She was fast as lightning. Quick as a wolf. Nimble as a fox. And an old, sweaty man brandishing a broom was not going to get rid of her.

"But I'm telling the truth," Nim said as she darted away from the broom. "I swear it's the truth. Please, just let me buy some food. A silver given by a tattercoat is worth the same as a silver given by a lady."

"I don't trade in stolen goods," the storekeeper growled.

"Fine." If the man wasn't going to be nice to Nim, she wasn't going to be nice to him. "If you won't let me buy anything, I'll steal it instead. And I'll tell all the other tattercoats to come in here and steal things too."

After all the sweeping and hitting and darting, Nim now stood behind the counter, right in front of the register, which held the day's earnings.

"Don't you dare," the storekeeper said.

"Oh, I will," Nim replied. After four years on the streets, she knew that if manners weren't getting you anywhere, your next best bet was a threat, even just an empty one.

Luckily for Nim, her empty threat worked. The storekeeper's face grew as pale as an unbaked strudel, and he dropped the broom.

"Please," he begged. "I can't have tattercoats running amok in here. I'll lose my customers."

"Then take my coin, give me two apple tarts, and I'll be on my way."

The storekeeper sighed and took the money. When Nim left the store, the change in her pocket jingled louder than the bell on the door.

"We'll keep most of these nickels for later," Nim said as she bit off a piece of the tart and handed it to Nibbles. "But I think we can spend a little bit more on something special for you."

While the tarts were still warm, Nim went to the tailor's and bought the finest square of fabric she could find. It had been two years since she'd last made a coat for Nibbles. It was now so frayed it was about to fall off.

Nim placed Nibbles on the cobbled ground. She draped the material—a soft sky blue—around his little neck. She'd stitch it into a coat tonight.

"Look at us," she said to her friend. "Nibbles and Nim: the grandest duo in Hodeldorf."

Nim held out her hand, and Nibbles stepped onto it. She was just rising to her feet when a voice spoke behind her.

"You'd be able to buy cloth even grander than that if you came with me."

Nim turned to see a pale girl standing behind her. The girl looked about the same age as Nim and was dressed in tatty clothes. Nim didn't recognize her, but when she saw the girl's hands were stained black, she immediately knew where she was from.

"You're not going to fool me," Nim said. She put Nibbles in her pocket and stepped away. "I know who you are. There's no way I'm going with you."

The girl scowled and tried to grab Nim. But Nim was too quick. She darted free of the girl's grip and raced off down the lane. The black-handed girl gave chase for a few minutes. But when she saw how fast Nim could run, she stopped.

The girl slumped against a streetlamp and looked mournfully around the empty street. Even if it had been full of children, she doubted any would have followed her. One glimpse at her hands and they ran away. But she couldn't give up. Everyone at the factory was relying on her. So she pulled herself off the streetlamp and went in search of another.

After her encounter with the black-handed girl, Nim decided it was time to go home. It was getting dark, and she never stayed out longer than the sun. In

Hodeldorf, there were thieves who thieved during the day and thieves who thieved during the night, and even a skilled daytime thief like Nim didn't want to bump into a nighttime one.

Nim turned onto Wintertide Lane. The streetlamps had been lit for the night. She darted around the pools of light and came to a stop outside a spindly brick house that was attached to two more.

Nim peered through the front window of house twenty-seven. A warm fire crackled inside. Helene and Minna Vidler played a board game beside the flames. Their parents, Hans and Hilda, kept watch from their armchairs.

"I think it's time for bed," Hans said to his two daughters. His voice trickled through the glass, so Nim could hear.

"Can't we play one more game?" Helene asked.

"Please, Papa?" Minna begged. "It's not fair. You always make us go to bed so early."

"It's true," Helene whined. She scrunched up her face and pretended to cry.

Nim rolled her eyes. Helene and Minna spent most of their time whining: whining that they didn't like their vegetables, whining that they had to go to bed, and whining when their mother combed their hair. Nim couldn't understand. If she had her own room with a fireplace and books and a snuggly bed and not just one parent but two, she'd never whine again.

When Minna pretended to cry as well, their father gave in.

"All right," he said. "You can play another game."

Hans rose from his chair and turned toward the window. Nim ducked and pressed herself against the brick wall. The light from the window faded as Hans closed the curtains.

Nim breathed a sigh of relief. Despite Nim's having lived above the family for four years, they had never seen her. Nim wanted to keep it that way. If they knew a tattercoat slept on their roof, they would take steps to get her off. They might throw rocks at her until she left. They might spray water onto the roof at night so she would slip off in the morning. Or they might hammer metal spikes between the tiles so she wouldn't be able to sit without piercing her bottom. That's what the Heiner family had done to Snot. Three weeks later, he was dead. But it wasn't the spikes that had killed him. It was Blink. Blink had betrayed Snot in the most horrible way a tattercoat could be betrayed. And he had never been forgiven.

Nim left the window and climbed the trellis that led up to the roof. Her toes left little marks in the snow as she tiptoed over to her chimney. She used the sleeve of her coat to wipe away a patch of snow. She sat down and pressed herself against the bricks. A faint feeling of heat trickled through her clothes and warmed her skin.

In the dying light of day, Nim took a needle, some thread, and a small pair of scissors from her bag. Using Nibbles's old coat as a guide, she stitched the rat a new one.

"My, don't you look fine?" Nim said when she had finished and Nibbles tried on his new coat. He rose onto his back legs and raised his nose smartly in the air. "You look even finer than Otto in his green coat."

At the mention of Otto, Nim wondered if the boy from Dortzig was okay. Even though Otto had gotten most of his money back, he didn't have a coat. Still, he had five silver coins, and once he found his mother, she would make him another coat even fancier than the first.

"Yes," Nim whispered to Nibbles as they settled down to sleep. "We don't need to worry about him. Anyone who can afford a coat that grand can surely afford another."

Nim had good reason to be worried about Otto that night. Only not for the reason she thought. There was a far greater danger lurking in the city than the cold. A danger that was heading right for him.

Otto couldn't believe his bad luck. First he'd lost

his mother. Then he'd lost his coat. And then he'd lost all his money. True, Nim had given most of the coins back, but it still hadn't been a pleasant experience.

"Good evening, Herr Kruger," Otto said when he arrived at the inn. After walking around the streets without a coat, he was desperate to get inside. A few hours sitting in front of the fire upstairs would surely warm him up. Tomorrow, he could use his coins to buy a new coat. Then he could keep searching for his mother.

"Almost two weeks' rent you owe me," Herr Kruger said. He stood on the front step, blocking Otto's entry.

"I know. I'll be able to pay it back just as soon as I find my mother."

Herr Kruger sighed and shook his head. "That's not good enough, Otto. I need to make a living. I can't let you stay here for free."

"I won't stay for free. Here." Otto pulled out his coins. "You can have all of my money, and I can work to cover the rest. I can help in the kitchen. I can clean. I can do whatever you need me to do. Please, Herr Kruger. I don't have anywhere else to stay."

Herr Kruger took the coins. They didn't cover the full amount Otto owed.

"I'm sorry, Otto. I don't need the help, and besides, I rented out your room to another guest this morning.

They've paid three weeks in advance. I'll keep your belongings in a safe place. Once you find your mother, you can come and collect them."

"But where will I go?" Otto said.

"Do you know anyone in the city?"

Otto shook his head. "I only met one person today, and she was a thief. Please. Can't I stay for just a while longer? I'll sleep on the floor. I'll sleep anywhere."

Herr Kruger laughed a sad laugh. "Look," he said. "I've rented out all of my rooms, and I can't have you sleeping in the common areas. It would be bad for business. But there's an alley behind the inn. It's quiet and dark, and some of the heat from the kitchen keeps it warm. You can stay there until you find your mother."

Herr Kruger stepped inside and closed the door. Otto turned away and walked over to the alley. It wasn't the most welcoming place. It was cold, the cobbles were hard, and he no longer had a coat to keep him warm. But at least no one was there to bother him or rob him.

Otto kicked away a section of snow and lay down. He curled up in a tight ball to protect himself against the cold. He couldn't believe this was how things had ended up. His father was dead, his mother was missing, he was homeless in a strange city, and his coat had been stolen. He couldn't think of a single positive thought. Eventually, exhaustion lulled his eyes closed.

Only moments later, a voice woke him up.

"Are you okay?" someone said.

Otto jumped with fright. A girl stood over him, holding a lantern that lit the alley. Her hair was plaited and tied together with black ribbon. The ribbon didn't look like the ribbons his mother owned. It wasn't smooth and shiny. It was thick and flaky, like the color came from grime instead of dye.

"You don't look okay," the girl continued. "You look cold and sore and tired."

"That's because I am," Otto said. This was the first time in over a week that someone had noticed how upset he was. He realized just how much he wanted someone to talk to. Since his mother had disappeared, he'd barely spoken to anyone aside from that girl Nim and her rat. "And that's not the worst of it. I've also lost my mother. She disappeared, and I've been looking for her ever since."

"That's awful," the girl replied. "But I think I know someone who could help."

"Really?" For the first time in days, Otto felt hope rise inside him. Despite his not having a coat, the world seemed to grow a little warmer.

The girl nodded. "I can take you to her right now. She doesn't live far away. She's probably still awake as well, wondering where I've got to. Come on," the girl said. She held out her hand. "She'll be able to find your mother in no time."

Though skeptical this unknown person could help, Otto was tired and desperate and freezing. He was willing to try anything to find his mother. After all, if he had been the one to go missing, she would have torn the whole city apart to find him.

"Okay," Otto said. He reached out and took the girl's hand. She helped him up, and they walked off down the lane. Perhaps because he was so tired, or perhaps because he had been looking at the girl's pale face and nowhere else, Otto did not notice that the hand he held was stained black.

Chapter Five

FRAU FERBER'S FACTORY

"It's not much farther," the girl with the lantern said as she led Otto through the darkness.

Otto hoped it wasn't. They had been walking for at least half an hour. They'd left Herr Kruger's Inn far behind, and they were now near the outskirts of the city. The coldness that covered Hodeldorf during the day was even worse at night. His skin had gone numb, and he couldn't feel a thing.

"Do you really think this lady can help?" Otto asked as they walked.

"Absolutely," the girl said. "Frau Ferber is very good at finding things."

They turned down another street. Out of the corner of his eye, Otto saw two lanterns bobbing in the street behind them.

"I think someone's following us," he whispered, moving closer to the girl.

"Don't worry. That's Helmut and Heinz. Frau Ferber sent them to look after me. Now, here we are."

The girl stopped before a large brick building. Chimneys littered the roof, but no smoke puffed up into the night sky. The bricks and the windows were stained black. A brass sign was nailed to the front door: FRAU FERBER'S BOOT POLISH FACTORY.

The girl pointed to the third floor. Candlelight flickered through a large grimy window.

"That's Frau Ferber's study," she said. "I told you she'd still be up."

The two of them waited for Helmut and Heinz to catch up. They had the key to unlock the front door. It creaked open, and Otto was led inside.

The first thing Otto noticed about the boot polish factory was that it was warm: warmer than anywhere else in the city. It was even warmer than Dortzig. Then he noticed the smell: oil and dirty people. The floorboards were rotten, and Otto could see old gray rats scurrying about in the shadows.

"Maybe I should go." Otto turned toward the door, but Helmut had already locked it.

"You can't go now," the girl said. "We're almost there."

Otto was led up the staircase. It was as rotten

as the floor. With every step, he feared he would fall straight through the moldy wood.

They stepped onto the second floor. It was dark and silent. But it was a strange silence: the kind of silence where you couldn't hear anything, not because there was nothing to hear but because whoever or whatever was there was too afraid to make a sound.

They climbed to the third floor. A thin line of warm light trickled out from a door to their right. Heinz knocked on the door, and a woman called them inside.

Frau Ferber's study took up one side of the building. Large windows on three sides looked out over the city. A little lady dressed in black sat behind a large wooden desk. A fireplace lay empty behind her. Despite there being no crackling fire, it was warm up here as well: not as warm as it was on the floors below, but still far warmer than the world outside.

"Well done, Bertha," the lady said. "I didn't think you had it in you."

The girl standing beside Otto smiled.

"How did you get him to come?" Frau Ferber asked.

"I told him you would help find his mother. He's lost her, you see."

"Is that so?" Frau Ferber turned back to Otto.

Otto nodded. "She disappeared two weeks ago,

and I've been searching for her ever since. Bertha said you might be able to help me find her."

"Perhaps I can." Frau Ferber turned back to Bertha. "Congratulations. You're free to go."

"Thank you, Frau Ferber." Bertha smiled at the lady and turned toward the door. As her eyes fell upon Otto, a flicker of guilt crossed her face. Then she was gone.

"Now . . ." Frau Ferber turned back to Otto. "I'll get started on finding your mother first thing in the morning. You can stay here until we find her. You'll have a roof over your head and food every night. I'm sure you will find it quite pleasant after your nights on the street. A luxury, I should think. Now, Helmut, take him to his room."

The tallest boy led Otto to the second floor. He couldn't believe his luck. Not only had he found a warm place to sleep, but he'd also met someone who could help him search for his mother. As they walked down the rickety stairs, Otto asked where Bertha went.

"She left."

"The factory?"

Helmut nodded.

"Is she coming back?" Otto asked.

"Not if she can help it."

They stepped onto the second-floor landing.

"What do you mean?" Otto asked.

"Bertha's been trying to escape the factory for years. None of us thought she could do it. No one in Hodeldorf's gullible enough to trade places with one of Frau Ferber's children."

"What do you mean, 'trade places'?" Otto asked.

"Exactly what I said." Helmut opened the door. It led to a dark room. "In you go."

Otto felt a chill run up his spine. "I think I've made a mistake. I can find my mother by myself." Otto edged away from the room, but a hand pushed him forward.

"Oh no you don't," Heinz said. He had followed them from the third floor in case there was trouble. "The trade's been done. You belong to Frau Ferber now." He shoved Otto into the room and closed the door.

At first, Otto couldn't see a thing. He used his hands to feel his way around the space. Everything felt grimy and sticky, like even the walls and floors were trying to trap him and stop him from leaving.

Slowly, Otto's eyes adjusted. Moonlight trickled through the barred window and revealed a large room. The rotting wooden floor was covered in several rows of straw mattresses. Small lumps lay upon all except one. When one of the lumps moved, Otto realized they were children.

"Bertha?" one of the children said. She sat up and looked toward Otto. She saw his faint outline in the darkness and said, "I'm sorry you didn't find anyone."

"There's always next year," a boy added cheerfully.

"It's not Bertha," Otto said. "I'm Otto. Helmut said I've traded places, but I don't know what that means."

Several of the children gasped.

"I can't believe she did it," someone said.

"It's finally happened," whispered another.

"This is amazing," said a third. "Finally, we're going to be free."

The boy who had first spoken to Otto left his mattress and came over to shake his hand.

"I'm Gunter," he said.

"And I'm Frida," said the girl who had mistaken Otto for Bertha.

One by one, the other children introduced themselves. There were nineteen all up. Some were only a few years old, while others appeared older than Otto. They were pale and thin and dressed in rags, and their arms and hands were stained black.

Only one person in the room didn't introduce himself. He was an older boy sitting in the far corner.

"Don't mind him," Gunter said. "We call him Mouse, because he's as quiet as one. He can't speak. Doesn't have a tongue."

"What happened to it?" Otto asked.

"Frau Ferber cut it out because he whined too much," a boy called Klaus said.

Otto's eyes widened with fear. All the children, apart from Mouse, laughed.

"I get it," Otto said. "You're joking."

"Maybe." Gunter grew serious again. "Or maybe not. Mouse has worked in the factory longer than all of us. He's never been able to tell us what happened. All we know is he keeps a good distance from Frau Ferber and always passes the counting."

"What's that?" Otto said.

"Don't worry. You don't need to know about that. We'll be out of here before the next one. We might even be out of here tonight."

At that moment, a deep rumbling filled the room, and the walls of the factory shook.

"What's happening?" Otto asked.

"Just the factory," Gunter said. "It does that sometimes. Don't worry, you'll get used to it."

Otto didn't want to get used to it. It felt like the factory was alive. Maybe the walls really were trying to grab him.

"Are there any other children here?" Otto asked.

"Only Helmut and Heinz," Gunter said. "But they don't sleep in here with us. They're Frau Ferber's sons. She's going to leave the factory to them when she dies. I'm surprised they haven't killed her already. They're not very nice."

"I've noticed," Otto said. "What about you guys? Is Frau Ferber your mother as well?"

"Of course not!" Frida said.

"No way!" yelled a few of the other children.

"Then why do you live here?" Otto asked.

Most of the children fell silent; they didn't want to share their stories. But Gunter did.

"My mother sent me here because she couldn't feed me. She thought I'd be safe here, and warm. If she knew what Frau Ferber was really like, she would come and get me. Until today, we had no way of telling her. But now Bertha's going to tell everyone the truth. Once she does, our parents will come and save us. Soon, we'll all be going home."

Bertha couldn't believe it. After five years trapped inside the boot polish factory, she was finally going to be free. This was the moment she had been dreaming of. No more quotas and countings and punishments. No more sleeping on straw and working from before dawn to after dusk. Only one thing stood in her way. She needed the key to the front door.

Bertha waited patiently by the door for several minutes. She twirled her black ribbons while she waited. When she first came to the factory, they had been red, but the boot polish had slowly robbed the color away. When no one came to open the door, she began to climb back up the stairs.

"What are you still doing here?" Helmut asked when he bumped into her on the second floor.

"The door's locked. I can't get out."

"Oh. I forgot about that. Come on."

Helmut and Bertha walked back down to the ground floor. Helmut was just putting the key into the front lock when they were interrupted.

"What do you think you're doing?" Frau Ferber asked.

"Letting Bertha out, Mother."

"Why would you do that?"

"Because you said she could go." Helmut suddenly looked unsure of himself. He pulled the key away from the lock.

Frau Ferber shook her head. "Just because I say something, Helmut, doesn't mean I mean it. You're just as bad as Bertha. Maybe I should get you to fill the jars as well."

"So you don't want Bertha to leave?"

"Of course I don't want her to leave!" Frau Ferber stormed down the stairs and whacked Helmut over the back of the head. "No one leaves my factory!"

"But . . ." Bertha said.

"But what?" Frau Ferber snarled.

"But I found someone to take my place."

"I don't care. No one leaves my factory."

Helmut grabbed Bertha's arm and began to drag her up the stairs.

"Not that way," his mother yelled. "Take her downstairs."

Bertha's face paled.

"Please don't take me to the cellar," she said. "I haven't done anything wrong."

"Don't worry, dear," Frau Ferber said. "You're not going to the cellar. You're going somewhere else."

Helmut pulled Bertha over to the cupboard below the stairs. He pushed a piece of paneling aside to reveal a hidden door.

Bertha tried to run away. She slipped free of Helmut's grasp for a moment, but then he grabbed her by the hair and hauled her back. One of her ribbons fell onto the black floor. She opened her mouth to scream, but before she could, Helmut wrapped his hand over her mouth and dragged her into the darkness.

Chapter Six

THE FINEST BOOT POLISH
IN THE LAND

Otto woke to the same darkness he had fallen asleep in. His mattress was so thin he could feel the floorboards beneath it. As much as he'd hated the alley behind Herr Kruger's Inn, now he couldn't dream of anything better. Even sleeping on the streets was nicer than being locked in here. He really hoped Bertha was quick to spread the word about the factory. He didn't want to spend another night inside these grimy walls.

"Up!" Heinz yelled. "Get up!" He threw open the door to their room. He held a black truncheon thicker than Otto's leg. "Get up and get downstairs."

The children climbed off their mattresses. In the same clothes they'd slept in, they headed downstairs.

Thin tendrils of morning light trickled through the grimy windows on the ground floor. Two long tables ran the length of the room. At the end of each table was a large vat, with a smaller desk beside it.

"Line up," Heinz yelled.

The children ran to their places at the tables. Otto was directed to Bertha's old spot, standing between Gunter and Klaus.

Hundreds of empty glass jars covered the table, and a black bucket rested in front of each child, along with a large wooden crate. Both were empty.

Heinz looked at a large clock on the wall. It was six a.m. He thumped his stick on the ground and yelled, "Begin!"

One by one, each child picked up his or her bucket and used a tap on the side of the largest vat to fill it with sticky black paste. They returned to their places at the table and, for the next hour, carefully used their hands to scoop the black paste from their bucket and into the glass jars.

"What is this stuff?" Otto asked Gunter.

"Boot polish," he replied. He tried not to move his mouth, in case Heinz or Helmut were looking. "It gets sent all over the country by train. It's so good, even kings use Frau Ferber's polish."

Ironically, none of the other children in the factory had any shoes, except for Heinz and Helmut. They both wore black boots: they were the shiniest boots Otto had ever seen.

"Move your hands faster," Gunter whispered to Otto. Heinz was coming over to inspect their work. "If you move too slow, they'll whack you."

Otto's hands became a blur as he scooped handful after handful of the boot polish into the jars. When Heinz had moved on, Gunter continued.

"And don't forget to move your feet. If you stand still for too long, the rats'll start nibbling at your toes."

At the mention of rats, Otto's feet moved even faster than his arms.

"Slow down," Gunter whispered. "You'll never be able to keep that up all day."

"All day?" Otto said.

Gunter nodded.

"But what about breakfast? Don't we get to eat?"

Gunter looked at Otto strangely. "Frau Ferber doesn't believe in breakfast."

"But she told me I would be fed here."

"Only dinner," Klaus said. "And only if you reach the quota."

"What's that?"

"The number of jars you have to fill each day. The quota's set at three hundred."

"Three *hundred?*" Otto's mouth fell open. He'd

never be able to fill that many. "What about water?" he asked. "Do we at least get that?"

"You could scoop some out of the second vat." Gunter nodded to the vat they had yet to approach. "But it isn't very fresh, and it'll stain your teeth black for days."

"What about a break?" Otto asked. "Does Frau Ferber believe in those?"

"Oh yes," Gunter replied. "After one year of service, you get a day off to spend upstairs."

"That sounds nice," Otto said. "What do you get to do up there?"

"Just sleep in our room. Frau Ferber says it's very important to take time to rest. It's my third rest day next week," he said proudly. "And we get our birthdays off too. That's when we're allowed outside. If we can find someone to take our place, we get to leave. Frau Ferber calls it our birthday present."

Otto realized he had been Bertha's birthday present. He really hoped she told someone about what was going on in the factory so they would be freed. If she didn't, he would have been sent in here for nothing.

After they had filled all the jars on the table, they washed their hands in the second vat. Despite his rubbing between each of his fingers, a black residue remained on Otto's hands.

When everyone was finished washing, they screwed

the lids on the jars and covered each pot with a piece of oil paper that read: FRAU FERBER'S EXEMPLARY BOOT POLISH: NOTHING ELSE WILL MAKE YOUR SHOES SHINE AS BRIGHT.

Then they stacked their jars in a crate and began the whole process again.

It was dark by the time they stopped working. They had filled jars for thirteen hours. Otto was ready to sleep, but he still had to sit through the counting.

The counting was held in the same room they filled the jars in. Helmut sat at the small table beside the vats. He pulled a ledger from one of the locked drawers and opened to a page marked with a piece of thread. Then he called the first child forward.

Frida hauled her crate to the desk. Her arms shook under the weight. She looked happy about this. The heavier the crate, the closer you were to passing the counting.

"Three hundred and sixty-one jars," Helmut said when he'd counted them all. He marked the number beside her name in the ledger and said, "Good work."

One by one, the children were called forward. When Gunter approached the table, he looked nervous. But luckily, he scraped through with three hundred and five jars.

"That was close," he said to Otto when he returned to their table. He gave a nervous laugh.

Otto was the last to be called. Even though he had never been to a counting before, he knew just by watching the other children that he had failed to reach the quota. He'd been slow to fill his bucket with paste, and he still hadn't gotten the hang of putting it into the jars.

Helmut was quick to verify Otto's fear. He counted the jars and said with a smirk, "One hundred and eighty-six. That's a fail, Otto. No dinner for you."

As if on cue, Otto's stomach rumbled. He hadn't eaten anything for over a day. If he didn't eat tonight, he'd have to wait another full day before he got the chance to eat again. Considering how slow he was at filling the jars, he had a strong suspicion he would fail tomorrow night as well. At this rate, he would starve to death in a week.

Frau Ferber's children ate dinner at the same table they worked at.

"What is that stuff?" Otto asked when a bowl was placed in front of Gunter along with a thin slice of bread.

"Water mostly," Gunter said. "With a bit of cabbage thrown in. If we're lucky, there might even be some carrot. And once, I swear there was rabbit in there. Though Klaus swears even more it was rat."

"Well, it was," Klaus objected. "I found a tail."

"I don't understand why it's always so bad," Frida said. "Frau Ferber has fresh food delivered to the factory each week. A whole truckload of meat comes in, but none of it ends up with us. I've got no idea where it goes."

"I do," Gunter said. "It goes to them and their mother." He nodded to Helmut and Heinz. They were watching from the corner of the room, but they weren't touching any of the food.

For a moment, Otto was glad he hadn't passed the counting. The food looked disgusting. But once everyone else started eating, his hunger returned. Exhausted from a day of constant work, he needed to eat almost as much as he needed to sleep.

"Don't worry," Gunter said. "Frau Ferber might not look after us, but we look after one another." He tore off half of his bread and dunked it in the soup. He passed it to Otto under the table.

"Thanks," Otto said. He checked to make sure Helmut and Heinz weren't watching and quickly shoved the food into his mouth.

The meal tasted even worse than Otto had imagined, like the cook had added a bucket of dirt to the soup to thicken it up. There was only one positive.

Otto was certain there was no rat, because there wasn't anything in there at all, apart from the water and dirt.

"Frau Ferber must have had a bad day," Gunter mumbled. "But"—he added optimistically—"at least she didn't take away the bread."

Chapter Seven

THE MELTING SLIPPER

The tattercoats left their chimneys at dawn and slipped down onto the quiet streets below. Early in the morning, the air was so still and clear you could see all the way to the woods.

When Nim was little, she had always wanted to venture into the woods surrounding Hodeldorf. But then she'd heard some truly terrible stories—stories of people going into the woods and never coming out—and her dreams of venturing beyond the city walls disappeared.

With nickels to spare, Nibbles and Nim headed to the main square, where they bought pancakes for breakfast. Unless someone dropped one on the ground, they never usually got to eat them. It was a special treat to have a warm pancake that wasn't covered in dirt.

While they ate, Nim saw several other tattercoats

darting about the square stealing their own breakfasts: mostly bruised fruit that no one would buy or scraps they found on the cobbled ground.

If you had your eyes peeled for tattercoats in Hodeldorf, you'd see them all around, but most people looked the other way. Nim wasn't upset about this. She found it quite handy. It was a lot easier to steal things—like food and matches and milk—when people weren't looking.

By the time the city was awake, Nim had only one nickel left.

"We'll save this for later," she said to Nibbles. The morning was so cold, he had yet to rise from her pocket. Even the scent of freshly cooked pancakes hadn't been enough to lure him out. She'd had to drop pieces in for him to gobble up. "Besides, we don't need to buy anything else today. We already have everything we need. We each have a coat, a stomach full of pancakes, and a friend for constant company. We're doing pretty well for ourselves, aren't we?"

Nibbles was still hiding away from the cold when Nim spotted two of her favorite tattercoats.

Skid and Roe were busy stealing a patch of cloth to mend their old coats when they noticed Nim watching. While the tattercoats may have gone unnoticed by most of the city folk, they never went unnoticed by one another. They came over to say hello.

"Morning, Nim," Skid said cheerfully. Skid was a short boy who had high hopes for himself: high hopes he would grow to be as tall as the man whose coat he'd stolen. Unfortunately, his hopes had yet to come true, and he needed to hitch the coat up with rope so he didn't trip over it.

"Hi, Skid," Nim said. "Nibbles says 'Morning' too, only he can't be bothered to get out of my pocket today."

"I couldn't be bothered to get up from my chimney either," said Roe. "It feels like the cold in Hodeldorf is always getting colder." As if to ward the cold away, Roe had decorated her coat with scraps of material cut into the shape of suns. Most of the suns had faded to gray, but a few still held a semblance of color and sparkled in the weak light of the day.

Nim would have sewn a few suns into her own coat if she'd thought it would make a difference. But she knew Hodeldorf would still be cold even if she wore a coat full of suns.

Once Skid and Roe had snatched their own breakfast, they walked with Nim to an old alley near the train station. The alley was filled with all sorts of broken things—chairs with missing legs, rickety tables, and cupboards without doors or shelves—that the tattercoats had found discarded in the streets and fixed up. When they arrived, almost twenty other tattercoats were already there.

Over the years, the group of homeless children had remained steady at about thirty members. When a coldstorm hit, a few tattercoats would die and a few others would join the group. If the city were warm, there probably wouldn't have been any need for the group. But the cold kept robbing their parents away—along with a few other things—and if they didn't become tattercoats, there was only one other place they could go: Frau Ferber's factory.

"Morning, Sage," Nim called as she sat beside the others.

"Good morning, Nim," Sage replied with a cheerful wave.

Sage was currently the oldest tattercoat. She'd joined the group at the age of eight, when a coldstorm killed her father. A sickness had killed her mother the year before. Seven years later, she was the leader of the group.

Most of the tattercoats came from poor families, who couldn't afford to keep a fire burning through the cold. Sage was poor too, but when she joined the group, she could already read and write. By the age of ten, she'd written down the Tattercode: a set of rules developed by the founders of the group to keep everyone in line. At the age of eleven, she'd begun to teach the other tattercoats how to read it. Now she gave lessons in writing it.

Nim and the other tattercoats gathered as Sage began the day's lesson.

Every lesson started the same way: the tattercoats would write the Tattercode. Nim was almost as quick with a pen as she was with her feet. She nimbly wrote the five rules down:

THE TATTERCODE

RULE 1—You must choose your own name.

RULE 2—You must always help a tattercoat in need.

RULE 3—You must steal only what you need, not what you want.

RULE 4—You must not leave a trail, or else you will get caught.

RULE 5—You must own only one coat at a time. You can get a new coat only when your old one has turned to tatters.

Nim checked all the words to make sure she had spelled them right. Then she showed them to Sage.

"Very good, Nim," she said with an approving nod. "I think you'll be able to teach your own lessons soon."

"Really?" Nim said. She'd like that.

When the other tattercoats had finished, Nim asked Sage to tell them a story. Sage knew hundreds of them: stories about giants who left the woods and trampled the city, stories about witches who turned princes into frogs, and stories about princesses who were never happy, no matter how many wishes they got.

"All right," Sage said. She loved telling stories as much as the younger tattercoats loved listening to them. "Have you heard the one about the prince of Hodeldorf?"

"We don't have a prince," Nim said.

"Not anymore," Sage corrected.

*T*wo hundred years ago, the king of Hodeldorf held a magnificent ball for his only son. He invited the finest ladies in the land to attend. At the end of the ball, the prince was going to choose a wife.

The ball began at dusk. One by one, the ladies arrived. The prince greeted each one at the steps to the castle.

"Good evening, Lady Lang," he said to the first maiden who arrived. She wore a fine blue dress and a necklace that glinted in the light of the setting sun.

"Good evening, Lady Wolff. You do look splendid tonight," he said to the second maiden.

The prince had greeted one hundred maidens—all the ladies his father had invited to the ball—and was about to enter the castle when he heard the clink of distant but approaching horseshoes.

In the lamplight, a silver carriage appeared. It was drawn by six white horses adorned with feathered plumes. The carriage stopped before the prince, and a lady stepped out.

She wore a splendid dress, with silk stockings, pearl earrings, and diamond slippers. She was the most beautiful woman the prince had ever seen, but strangely, she didn't have an invitation. So as taken with her beauty as he was, the prince invited her inside nonetheless. She said her name was Lady Snow.

Under the sparkling light of four hundred chandeliers, the prince and the lady in the diamond slippers shared one and then two and then three dances. The other ladies realized the prince had already chosen his wife. So, while the prince and his chosen lady continued to dance, the other ladies gorged on the fine feast that had been prepared for them.

They shoveled whole pheasants into their mouths and soaked the gravy up with the frills on their dresses. They guzzled rose-hip wine and slurped up elderberry jelly. They tore apart the cherry-and-cream pie, and while they ate the dessert with their hands, they cursed the maiden who had come to the ball without an invitation.

The clock tower chimed ten and then eleven. As it neared midnight, the prince prepared to make an announcement. By now the hall had grown very warm. As Lady Snow spun 'round and 'round, droplets of water began to fall onto the floor.

It was then that the other ladies realized Lady Snow wasn't wearing fine pearls and expensive diamonds. She was dressed in frozen water shaped into jewels. Their awe turned to laughter, and they pointed at Lady Snow as her finery melted away.

In shame, Lady Snow fled from the castle. She jumped into her carriage and disappeared into the night.

While the ladies laughed, the prince ran after Lady Snow. He called out her name, but she was too upset to hear. As the clock tower chimed midnight, the castle began to swing and shake. The chandeliers hanging from the ceiling rattled and swayed. Candles, still alight, crashed to the ground. Then the glass chandeliers themselves began to topple to the floor. The windows of the castle shook, and then the castle itself. The crowd began to scream with fear. An earthquake was striking the city.

The ladies and the prince and the king and the queen fled from the crumbling castle. All around them, they watched the great monuments of the city tumble down. Down crashed the cathedral. Down crashed the clock tower. And down crashed Hodeldorf Castle. By the time the ground stilled, half the city had fallen.

"I bet it was Lady Snow," one of the maidens said.

"She probably wasn't even a lady," said another. "She was a witch who came to curse the castle and our wonderful prince."

By the time dawn arrived—slightly later than the day before—everyone in the city believed witchcraft was behind the great disaster. Everyone except the prince, that is. He set out to find his love, looking for years and years, until finally, after a decade of searching for the beautiful lady in the melting slippers, the prince of Hodeldorf gave up. In grief, he left Hodeldorf and never returned.

But the most curious thing about that night wasn't the mysterious guest or the earthquake that made the city fall. The strangest thing was that it was warm. Not warm from the heat of fires burning in the night. It was so warm that no

*fires had even been lit. It was, as the people back
then had called it, a time known as summer.*

*During summer, the sun shone brighter and
the nights grew shorter. There was no snow or icy
wind. Instead, a warm breeze floated throughout
the city. It was so warm—both day and night—
that no one even needed a coat.*

When Nim heard this last bit of the story, she
started to laugh. The other tattercoats did as well.

"Well, that's just silly, Sage," Nim said. "Maybe
not the earthquake bit"—for she had felt a few little
tremors herself over the years—"but definitely the part
about the coat. No one in Hodeldorf would ever go
outside without one of those."

"But it's true," Sage said. "Years ago, long before
any of us were born, the whole city was warm. Then,
the coldstorms began and summer disappeared. Now
every year is colder than the one before."

"How come?" Nim asked.

"No idea." Sage paused for a moment and then
said, almost to herself, "Maybe Lady Snow really did
curse the city."

Nim doubted that. Curses were like magic. They
weren't real. Something else was behind the cold, but
what?

Chapter Eight

THE COUNTING

As each day passed in Frau Ferber's factory, a sense of dread grew heavier upon Otto. Not only had he failed every daily quota, but he was no closer to finding out what had happened to his mother. He couldn't believe he had been tricked by Bertha. He should have been searching every street and every home for his mother; instead, he was filling stupid jars with stupid boot polish, and he wasn't even good at it.

Otto's mind was filled with another fear. He'd been in the factory for a week. A lot could change during that time. His mother could have come back. What if she had been lost or stuck somewhere but had now returned to Herr Kruger's Inn? What if she thought Otto had left? What if she'd given up on him and gone back to Dortzig? How would she ever find him here?

Otto's sense of despair was shared by the other children, only for a different reason. Bertha had left the factory a week ago. If she had said something about the factory, someone would have freed them by now. Wouldn't they? Either something had happened to her so she couldn't tell anyone the truth, or she'd never planned to help them at all. Otto couldn't decide which would be worse. He didn't want Bertha to be hurt or injured, but he also didn't want to have been lured into this factory for nothing. Something must have happened to her. But what?

At the end of each week, Helmut and Heinz took the ledger up to their mother's office. The children waited in their room for their names to be called. Unlike the daily counting, where most of the children looked confident, every child looked frightened before the weekly counting.

"The daily quota's always the same, but the weekly one changes," Gunter explained. "Sometimes it's three thousand jars, sometimes it's four thousand, and if Frau Ferber's having a bad week, she might make it five thousand. No one's ever passed that one. Even if you pass every daily quota, you could still fail the weekly one."

"But that's not fair," Otto said.

"But it's fun," Klaus replied. "At least it's fun for Frau Ferber."

"Don't be too worried," Gunter said when he saw the look on Otto's face. "Everyone is punished eventually."

One by one, the children were called into Frau Ferber's study. If they passed the counting, they returned to the room. If they failed, they were led back to the factory floor to await their punishment.

The weekly counting took a lot longer than the daily one.

"That's because Frau Ferber likes to make us wait," Frida said before she was called into the office.

A further hour passed before it was Otto's turn to enter. So far every child called into the study had passed and returned to their room. Helmut told Otto to be silent so Frau Ferber could read out his numbers.

"Hmm," Frau Ferber said as she looked down at the ledger. "My, my. It hasn't been a good week for you. You haven't passed a single daily counting." She looked up from the ledger and smiled. "You must be awfully hungry."

"I'd probably still be hungry even if I had passed the countings," Otto mumbled.

"You don't think I feed you enough?" Frau Ferber said.

"You haven't fed me anything," Otto pointed out. Luckily, the other children had. Each day a different one would share their meal with him so he didn't starve. The best thing about the factory was all the kind children inside it.

"You like to talk back, don't you?" Frau Ferber said. "I'd stop doing that if I were you. The last boy who talked back hasn't talked again."

"Mouse?" Otto said. He thought of the boy who sat in silence day in and day out. Otto sealed his lips shut.

Frau Ferber smiled and looked back down at the ledger.

"I'm awfully sorry, Otto, but you've failed to make the counting: over four hundred jars off. You'll have to pick up the pace next week."

Frau Ferber nodded to Heinz, who led Otto downstairs.

At first, Otto was all alone on the factory floor. He would have opened a window and jumped out into the night if he could have. But he knew that would be pointless. The bars on the windows were even thicker than Heinz and Helmut's truncheons.

As the minutes passed, Otto feared he would face the punishment alone, so it was almost a relief when he heard a set of footsteps coming down the stairs. His heart fell when he saw who the footsteps belonged to. Gunter had also failed the counting.

"I don't understand," Otto said. "How did you fail?"

"It's my hands," Gunter said. "They're getting too big. Soon, they won't be able to fit inside the jars."

"What happens then?" Otto asked.

"I'm out," Gunter said sadly.

"Isn't that good?"

"I don't mean out on the streets," Gunter said. "Out somewhere else."

"Where?"

"No one knows. Once your hands are too big, you disappear—and never come back. Some say Frau Ferber sells us for a profit: one nickel for each ounce. Some say she melts us down into boot polish. And some say she dumps us in the woods for the wolves to eat."

At the mention of the woods, Otto shivered. He could still remember the eerie feeling he had felt when he first arrived in Hodeldorf: the feeling that the trees around the city were full of evil things and the evil things were watching him. He tried not to let his fear show.

"Which one do you think it is?" he asked.

Gunter shrugged. "No idea. All I know for sure is this: once your hands get too big, you're called into Frau Ferber's office and you're never seen again."

At that moment, Helmut and Heinz entered the room.

"They supervise every punishment," Gunter whispered. "That's why they hate us slacking during the day. It means they miss out on a night in bed too."

Heinz fetched two buckets from the table.

"Eighty-two," he said to Gunter as he handed him one of the buckets.

"Four hundred and twenty-five," he said to Otto as he handed him the other.

"Huh?" Otto said.

"That's how many jars you need to fill before you can go to bed. You've got to reach the quota."

"But that'll take all night."

"Then you better learn to fill the jars a little quicker during the day."

"Don't worry," Gunter whispered to Otto as they went over to the vat of boot polish. "I should be finished in a couple of hours. Then I can help you."

"Won't you get in trouble?"

"By who? Those two?" He nodded to Heinz and Helmut, who were sitting at the far table. "They'll fall asleep within the first hour. If we work quickly, we might even get an hour or two of sleep before we have to start working tomorrow."

"Thanks, Gunter," Otto said, taken aback by this boy's willingness to help him.

They began filling the jars. For the first two hours, their hands moved swiftly. Gunter finished his jars and started to help Otto, but by midnight, they were both slowing down.

"We'll take turns," Gunter said. "You sleep for an hour while I keep working. Then we'll switch."

Otto gratefully rested his head on the table, and within minutes, he was fast asleep. When Gunter shook him awake, weak sunlight filtered through the window.

"What time is it?" Otto asked with a yawn.

"Almost seven." Gunter yawned as well.

"You didn't wake me." A sick feeling washed over Otto. "Did you fall asleep too?"

Gunter shook his head. "I finished filling the jars."

Otto looked at the table. Over five hundred labeled jars were stacked neatly in front of him.

"Why didn't you wake me?" he said to the older boy. "You didn't get any sleep."

"You needed it more than me. Besides, that's what we do in the factory. We help one another out."

For the first time since arriving at the factory, Otto felt almost grateful to be there. Sure, he was always starving. Sure, he was always tired. And, sure, he was always dirty. But he'd met Gunter here, and lots of other kind children too. He felt like he'd found a group of people he belonged with. He only wished they weren't locked inside a horrible factory. If they had been free on the streets, and if he'd had his mother back, he would have been happy.

Chapter Nine

OTTO'S TICKET
OUT OF THE FACTORY

The weeks passed in Frau Ferber's factory. Otto got the hang of filling the jars with polish and managed to pass the next three weekly countings. Gunter wasn't so lucky. He failed two and was forced to stay up filling jars for eight hours. By the time he was finished, his hands were bleeding, and throbbing with pain.

"I can barely feel my fingers," he said to Otto while they waited for another weekly counting. "And they've swollen up as well. Soon, they're going to be too big, and I'll be called into Frau Ferber's office and never seen again."

"They don't look too big to me," Otto lied. He'd managed to fill almost as many jars as Frida that week.

It had been a hard task; his hands were also swollen from the effort of pushing them in and out of the jars.

"Do you really think so?" Gunter asked hopefully. He held his hands out beside Otto's. They were almost the same size.

When Otto was called into Frau Ferber's office, he barely heard her say he had passed the weekly counting. His mind was on something else. When Helmut began to lead him from the room, he walked the other way.

"What do you think you're doing?" Frau Ferber said when Otto approached her desk.

"I wanted to know if you've had any luck finding my mother," Otto said.

Frau Ferber smirked. "It would be a miracle if I had."

"How come?" Otto asked.

"Because I haven't been looking for her." Frau Ferber's smirk turned into a smile. Several of her teeth were missing, or perhaps it only looked that way because they were black like everything else in the factory.

"Well, if you're not going to find my mother, I'd like to leave." Otto tried to sound brave, but he had a feeling he just sounded silly.

"Is that so?" Frau Ferber said.

"It is."

The smile that had touched the edges of Frau

Ferber's mouth disappeared. She stood up and said, "You're not a very smart lad, are you? Since you don't seem to understand what's happening, let me explain it to you. Your mother is either dead or she's abandoned you. Either way, she's not coming back, and she doesn't want you to find her. You're still a boy, and you have no one else in this world to look after you and keep you safe. That's why you're going to stay here in my factory and work for me."

"But I don't want to," Otto said.

"Lots of children don't want to eat their vegetables, boy. But they do because their parents tell them to."

"You're not my parent."

"I'm the closest thing you've got to a parent now. And as your parent, I'm telling you to go to bed. It's getting late, and you've got an early start in the morning."

"But I don't want to be here anymore," Otto said, fighting back the tears that were prickling his eyes. He moved closed to Frau Ferber. The next time he spoke, his voice was loud. "I want to leave."

"Where would you go?" Frau Ferber asked.

"I'm not sure yet. Why can't you just let me go? You let Bertha leave."

"That's because she found someone to replace her. That's how things work at my factory. No one leaves without first organizing a replacement."

"So if I trick someone into taking my place, I can leave too?"

"Of course. But you're only allowed out one day per year. And I'm afraid that day is on your birthday. So you'll have to wait before you can go out there." She nodded to the window. It was so grimy you could barely see through the glass.

"Well," Otto said, "it just so happens that my birthday's tomorrow."

Frau Ferber raised a skeptical eyebrow.

"Is that so?"

Otto nodded. "I'm turning twelve," he lied. He needed to get out of the factory; he needed to start searching for his mother again. The factory was sealed so tightly he knew the only way out was if Frau Ferber let him. "So, can I go?"

Frau Ferber thought about this for several seconds. Then she shrugged and said, "It makes no difference to me. You have all of tomorrow to find your replacement. But if you don't find anyone, you'll have to wait a full year before you can try again. And don't go getting any ideas," she warned. "You can't just run away and disappear. Heinz and Helmut will follow you, and if you try anything you shouldn't, you'll be sleeping in the cellar with the rats. There are thousands down there. They're so hungry I've heard they eat one another. They've even eaten one of the children. I bet they'd enjoy eating you too."

Otto hoped Frau Ferber was joking. But he had a feeling she wasn't. Maybe it wasn't such a good idea to leave the factory after all.

The following morning, while all the other children filled up their buckets with boot polish under the watchful gaze of Frau Ferber, Otto was led to the front door. Helmut and Heinz stood on either side of him.

"Remember what Mother said," Heinz warned. "If you try to run away, it'll be straight down to the cellar for you. The last person who went down there was never seen again."

Otto gulped and stepped outside. He knew the only way to escape Frau Ferber's factory was to find someone to take his place. And he had a very good idea who that someone would be. Otto walked the streets of Hodeldorf on the lookout for two people. He was looking for a girl in a tatty coat who owned a thieving rat, and a boy in a fine green coat that used to belong to him. If they hadn't robbed him, none of this would have happened.

Otto tried to make the most of his time outside the factory. He hadn't felt the sun in a whole month. The fresh air made him feel clean. It was awfully cold, though: far colder than inside the factory.

At first, Otto saw only adults as he walked the

streets of the city. He knew Frau Ferber wouldn't want one of them; their hands would be too large to fit inside the boot polish jars.

It was nearing noon when Otto spotted his first child of the day: a small boy dressed in a tatty coat. Before Otto had a chance to say hello, the boy spotted Otto's black hands and ran off down the road.

Lunchtime came and went. Otto's body had grown numb from the cold, and a deep hunger gnawed at his stomach. It felt like his body was trying to eat itself just to stay alive. Long shadows fell across the city. Otto searched every face in the main square but couldn't find the two he sought.

"Tick. Tock," Heinz said. The brothers had been keeping back until now, watching Otto from afar. "Time's running out."

"You're never going to find anyone," Helmut added. He was eating an apple. He crunched it right in Otto's face, so juice splattered across his cheeks. Otto was so hungry he almost licked it off. "You're the first person who's volunteered to go to the factory in ten years. No one else is going to be that stupid."

The two of them laughed and stepped back among the crowd. Otto ignored them and continued his search.

Despite spending the rest of the afternoon check-ing every corner of the main square, Otto still couldn't find the two people he sought. Night fell. It was almost time to head back to the factory. Knowing that once he stepped inside those walls he wouldn't get a chance to step back out for a year, Otto grew desperate.

"Excuse me," he called. He reached out for a girl who was passing by with her parents. They were several meters in front of her and didn't see their daughter turn.

"Can I help you?" the girl asked. She looked alarmed by how dirty he was but didn't move away.

"You can," Otto said. "You see . . ." He tried to search for the right words to get her to go to the factory. Before he could find them, the girl realized the stain on his arm wasn't just from dirt.

"Mother! Father!" she called. She raced away from Otto and back to her parents.

"Hello there," Otto said to two boys hurrying past the bakery. They were both younger than he was. Maybe if he brought two boys back, he could choose someone else to leave the factory as well. But his plans were ruined. The boys saw his stained hands before he'd finished his greeting, and raced off into the crowd.

When Otto spotted another boy wandering by himself, he shoved his hands into his pockets before calling out.

"Hi," he said, as cheerfully as he could.

"What's wrong with you?" the boy asked with a scowl.

"What do you mean?" Otto said, being careful to keep his hands hidden.

"Why are you so happy? What do you want?"

"Nothing, not really," Otto said. "Well, I was wondering if you wanted to go for a walk with me."

"Why would I want to do that?"

"Erm . . ." Otto couldn't think of an answer.

The boy shook his head and began to walk away.

Otto realized it was time to give up. Even if his hands were hidden, people wouldn't follow him. Besides, by now most of the people in the city had gone to bed. He turned to go as well and tripped over a small girl standing in the street.

"Sorry," he said, helping the girl back up. She didn't flinch when she saw his blackened hands. She must have been too young to know what they meant.

"That's okay."

"Are you lost?" Otto asked.

The girl nodded. "I was meant to hold my father's hand, but I let go, and now I can't find him. Could you help me?"

Otto couldn't believe his luck. It would be easy to take this girl back to Frau Ferber and trade her for his freedom. But at the very instant he knew this, he also knew he couldn't do it. It would be wrong.

"Go back to the main square and ask one of the stall owners. They should be able to help."

The girl thanked him and hurried off into the darkening night.

"You're even dumber than I thought," Heinz said as they walked back to the factory. "You had your ticket out of here, and you let it go."

"Now you're stuck inside for another year at least," Helmut added.

And that wasn't the worst of it, Otto thought as he trudged along the streets. While he'd been looking for Nim and Blink, he'd also been looking for someone else.

Otto had been searching the crowd for a woman with a red coat and an elm basket. But his mother wasn't there. Maybe Frau Ferber was right. Not about his mother abandoning him; he knew she would never do that. She loved him more than anyone else in this world. She used to tell him that every night before he went to sleep. But he was worried that maybe something horrible had happened to her: something so horrible that she was no longer alive. And if that was the case, maybe Frau Ferber was the closest thing to a parent he had left in this world.

This thought alone was enough to bring Otto to tears. He tried to hide them as he walked back to the factory.

Chapter Ten

THE FACE IN THE WINDOW

Nim was on a mission. She needed to steal something, and it was going to be difficult. Luckily, she knew just the thief for the job.

"Now, this is important," Nim said to Nibbles as they sat on the roof of the Vidlers' house. It was early in the morning, and the air was at its coldest. Nim's breath left her mouth in puffs of white. The fires blazing in the homes below were only coals at this time of day, so the smoke that usually shrouded the city was gone. Nim could see all the way to Hodeldorf Wood. "I need you to steal something very specific. It's something I've never stolen before because I've never needed it. But I think I need it now."

Despite being a rat, Nibbles seemed to understand. At the mention of the word *important*, he stopped nibbling on Nim's coat and listened very closely. His eyes didn't leave Nim's face as she explained the plan.

"We need to steal a pen," she said. Her old one had fallen through a hole in her coat pocket the day before. She needed a new one so she could continue her lessons with Sage.

This mission was difficult. Pens were usually kept in pockets. This meant Nibbles would have to sneak into someone's coat or pants and get a pen without being seen, without being felt, and, most important for Nibbles, without being squashed.

"Do you think you're up for it?" Nim asked.

Nibbles twitched his whiskers back and forth, as if weighing the pros and cons. Then he nodded.

"That's my Nibbles," Nim said. "Up for every challenge." She opened her coat pocket, and Nibbles dove inside. Then they set off.

The best place for stealing in Hodeldorf was the main square. When they arrived, the crowd was thin. Nim carefully stole an old, bruised pear from a fruit cart and shared it with Nibbles while they waited.

Finally, she spotted a rather grand-looking man in a black coat and matching top hat. "He looks the type to own a pen," Nim said, nodding to the man. "Don't you think?"

Before Nim had finished her sentence, Nibbles was off and after the prize. He scurried along the cobbles, darted between hundreds of feet, jumped onto the man's coat, and slipped underneath.

The man's coat moved up and down as if his own hand were searching for something. This continued for several seconds before Nibbles poked his head back out. His paw appeared a moment later. It was wrapped around a gold chain with a pen fastened to the end. But as Nibbles tried to pull the clasp free, the man began to yell.

"Argh!" he cried. "It's a rat: a blasted dirty gutter-living rat!" He slammed his fist down on his chest. He was quick, but not as quick as Nibbles; by the time the man touched his coat, Nibbles was already back on Nim's shoulder.

"Hmm," Nim said as they casually walked away. "That sure must have been a fine pen." She'd never seen one chained by gold before. "Never mind. We'll find someone else with a pen, just not as fine as that."

Nim searched the crowd until she spotted a man in a rather nice-looking fur coat. Nibbles spotted him too. Without a word, he was off. This time Nibbles didn't play around, and his pale tail quickly disappeared beneath the folds of the man's coat. A moment later, he reappeared with a thin black pen clutched triumphantly beneath his arm.

The weight of the pen slowed Nibbles down, but he soon made it back to Nim. The man didn't even know his pen had been taken.

"And that," Nim said, as she reached down and gave Nibbles a fond scratch behind his ears, "is why you're the second-best thief in the city."

"But still not the first," a boy whispered in Nim's ear.

Nim turned to see Blink crouched beside her. He was still wearing Otto's green coat. The hems of several other coats stuck out from beneath it. Blink smirked at Nim. Then, in a flash, he snatched the pen from Nibbles. Nim tried to snatch it back, but she was too slow.

"And I'm still quicker than you as well," Blink said to Nim. Then—in a blink, just like his name—he was off.

Nim knew there wasn't a moment to lose. She scooped Nibbles into her pocket and raced after the thieving little thief. Her legs were quick, quicker than most, but she quickly fell behind the boy she chased.

"Silly boy," Nim said as she darted after Blink. He was a flash of emerald green among a sea of gray. If he hadn't stolen such a fine coat, he would have been much harder to follow.

As if he had heard Nim's thoughts, Blink stopped. He tore off the green coat and stuffed it under his arm, and then set off again. This time, instead of being a blur of bright green, he was a blur of unremarkable brown. Still, Nim kept close behind as Blink left the main square. But no matter how quickly Nim moved her legs, Blink moved his even faster. It wasn't fair. Being weighed down by eight coats should have made him slower. As it was, the layers of material seemed to speed him up.

"We're never going to catch him," Nim said breath-lessly as she chased him down another alley. "Blink's faster than everyone." By now her lungs were aching in the cold air.

In the end, Nim need not have bothered. Blink got so far ahead that by the time she turned onto another street, he was long gone.

Nim leaned against a wall to catch her breath. When she pulled away, she noticed something sticky on her coat. Nim touched the stain. It made her fingers black. She jumped with fright.

So focused on catching Blink, Nim hadn't paid attention to where they were going. She stood before a black building with a brass sign on the door. Even with-out reading the words, Nim knew it said: FRAU FERBER'S BOOT POLISH FACTORY.

Nim knew this factory wasn't like any other fac-tory in the city. It wasn't a factory where grown-ups went to work during the day and left at night with a few coins in their pocket. This factory was full of children who never left at all and never got any coins for the work they did.

"Blasted Frau Ferber," Nim mumbled. She was

probably the only person in the city Nim hated more than Blink.

Nim wanted to get away as quickly as she could. But she was also curious to see beyond the factory walls.

The windows of Frau Ferber's factory were as grimy as the hands of the children who slaved away inside. Nim couldn't wipe the grime away, but through the dark haze she could make out the shapes of those on the other side.

Two long tables ran the length of the room, both cluttered with glass jars. Some were full, and others were empty. Nim counted twenty children busily trying to fill them all.

She was about to turn away when she spotted a familiar face among the workers. It was the boy who had owned the fine green coat.

As though he could sense Nim watching, Otto looked up. Their eyes locked. Sadness and anger flooded his face. Nim had to look away. She knew exactly how he felt, because once, she had sat at that same table.

Chapter Eleven

A NIBBLE IN THE NIGHT

Nim tried her best to forget the boy she had seen inside Frau Ferber's factory. She tried every trick she knew to keep her mind on other things. For the next two days, coats did not take up just one-quarter of her thoughts. They took up over three-quarters.

During the day, she looked at every coat she saw and memorized its features. At night, she fell asleep trying to recount the different colors and buttons and fur trims. And when she finally did fall asleep, all she dreamed about were coats.

But it didn't work. No matter which coat she fell asleep dreaming of, by the following morning she awoke to the thought of only one: that wondrous green coat and the boy who had owned it.

The truth was, Nim felt partly to blame for Otto's having ended up in the factory. Of course, she hadn't actually taken him there and locked him inside. But she couldn't stop thinking that if something had been different about their first meeting—if she had given all his silvers back or if she'd specifically warned him to keep away from children whose hands were stained black—he might never have ended up in there.

In the end, Nim realized there was only one way to get Otto off her mind. She would have to help him escape.

Otto was woken by a nibble on his toe. At first, he thought he was dreaming. But when the nibbles grew stronger and began to climb his leg, he knew he was wide-awake.

Otto kicked out his leg. The nibbling stopped, and he sat up in bed.

The other children remained asleep. Thin shards of moonlight shone through the blackened windows. In the faint light, Otto saw a small shape lying on the floor.

Despite the new coat he wore, the old gray rat lying motionless before him looked familiar. It was Nibbles: the thief who had stolen his coins.

Otto thought Nibbles was dead: that he'd killed

him when he kicked him across the room. But as he watched, the old rat opened his eyes and slowly sat up. With trembling whiskers, and his tail tucked between his legs, he looked up at Otto.

"What are you doing here?" Otto hissed. "If Nim sent you to rob me again, I'm awfully sorry, but I have nothing left for you to steal."

But instead of taking something from Otto, Nibbles handed him a small piece of rolled paper.

Otto took the paper from the rat's claws. A note was written on one side:

If you want to escape, go to the cellar.

"This is a trick, isn't it?" Otto said to Nibbles. "You and Nim are just as bad as Heinz and Helmut, possibly even worse. You're trying to send me to the cellar so I'm eaten by the rats." Otto's eyes widened with an idea. "That's what you were trying to do just now, weren't you? You were trying to eat my toe. Well, I'm not falling for this. Get out and go away."

On that note, Otto lay back down and closed his eyes. He needed as much sleep as he could get if he wanted to keep passing the counting. He didn't have time to waste on sneaky and cruel tricks.

Chapter Twelve

THE GIRL WHO WAS EATEN BY RATS

"Up," Heinz yelled as he opened the door. "Get up!"

Otto crawled off his mattress and stood.

"Good sleep?" Gunter asked.

Remembering his late-night visitor, Otto shook his head. The note had kept him awake for several hours. He was about to show it to Gunter when Heinz yelled at them again.

The children quickly raced out of the room.

"Not you." Heinz grabbed Gunter and pulled him back.

"Huh?" Gunter said. He hadn't done anything wrong. He'd gotten ready as quickly as the others, and he hadn't even been the last one out the door.

"Mother wants to see you in her study."

The chatter among the other children stopped. They all turned to Gunter. The older boy looked pale.

It always ended this way. You grew up in the factory, and your hands grew too. When they got too large, you'd get a tap on your shoulder. You'd be led up to Frau Ferber's office, and you were never seen again.

The children wanted time to say goodbye. They wanted to say they would miss Gunter. They wanted to say they didn't want him to go. Otto wanted to thank him for helping him and sharing his dinner when he was given none. But they didn't get that chance. Helmut marched them downstairs while Heinz led Gunter away.

"Maybe he'll come back," Otto said as he filled another jar with boot polish. He tried to ignore the way his own hand pushed against the rim of the jar. His fingers were growing almost too large to fit.

Klaus raised a skeptical eyebrow. Four days had passed since Gunter was taken to the third floor, and he hadn't been seen since. They all knew he wasn't coming back. They also knew if they didn't get out of the factory, they would eventually disappear as well.

To keep their minds off the loss, the children worked even harder at filling their jars. Otto was busy sticking labels onto his own when a shadow fell across one of the factory windows. He looked up and saw a girl staring back at him. A rat stood on her shoulder.

"Nim," Otto said through gritted teeth. She was the last person he wanted to see.

"What's that?" Klaus asked.

"Nothing." Otto looked back down at his jars.

Otto tried to focus on his work, but every few seconds his eyes were drawn up. The girl was still there. Eventually, Klaus noticed and followed Otto's gaze.

"Do you know her?" Klaus asked.

"Not really," Otto mumbled.

"She looks familiar," Klaus said.

"Did she rob you too?" Otto asked.

Klaus shook his head. "I've never been robbed, except by Frau Ferber."

"Well, she's a nasty girl," Otto said. "First she robbed me, and then she tried to trick me into going down into the cellar."

At the mention of the word *cellar*, Klaus's eyes flashed with wonder.

"What is it?" Otto asked.

"I remember now," he said. He looked at the girl in the window and then at Otto. "That's Elke."

"No, it isn't. That's Nim."

"Not when she was here, she wasn't. Remember, Frida?" He elbowed the girl sitting next to him. "She's the one who was sent to the cellar."

Frida glanced at the window.

"That's her, all right," she said. "We thought she'd died. Frau Ferber said she was eaten by the rats."

"What do you mean?" Otto asked.

"Elke lived in this place for years," Frida said. "Slept on the mattress next to me. She was one of Frau Ferber's best workers: had some of the quickest hands she'd ever seen. She was always trying to get out of here. One day, she tried to smash a window with her bucket. Frau Ferber was so angry she sent her to the cellar. When Heinz and Helmut went to let her out the next day, she was gone. We all thought she had been eaten by the rats. But maybe . . . she escaped."

That night, while Klaus and Frida distracted Heinz and Helmut with claims of an inaccurate counting, Otto slipped away from the table and sneaked over to the cellar door. If Frida and Klaus were right about Nim— if she had somehow escaped the factory from her place in the cellar—maybe her note wasn't a trick after all.

Otto tried to turn the door handle, but it wouldn't move. Even the cellar was kept under lock and key. He realized there was only one way to get in there. He would have to break the rules.

Chapter Thirteen

FRAU FERBER'S CELLAR

Otto didn't like breaking rules. But if breaking the rules meant he would escape Frau Ferber's factory and find his mother, he was willing to do it. And he knew just what rule to break.

The most valuable thing in Frau Ferber's factory was her boot polish. If one drop fell on the floor, a child was docked ten jars at the counting. This punishment wouldn't help Otto. He would have to spill far more to get the punishment he was after.

Otto had shared his plan with the other children and invited them to join in. But they were scared: so scared of what Frau Ferber would do. So Otto would have to do it on his own.

The day after he'd heard the story about Nim, that she used to be a girl called Elke, Otto woke early.

He was the first child down the stairs in the morning. He was the first child to line up at the vat of boot polish. And he was the first child to reach the tap. Only today, instead of filling his bucket with blacking paste, Otto threw it on the floor.

"Pick it up," Heinz said.

Otto ignored him. He reached out to the vat of boot polish and pushed against it with all his strength. The vat didn't move.

"Get back in line," Helmut warned.

Otto pushed against the vat again. But still, it wouldn't move. Otto feared his idea wouldn't work, but then one side of the vat lifted off the floor.

"Watch out!" Otto yelled to the children waiting in line.

Slowly, the vat rose higher. Frau Ferber's children raced to their tables and jumped up among the jars. A moment later, the vat thumped onto the ground. The walls of the factory shook, a section of rotted floorboard gave way, and a river of boot polish flooded out.

Black goop rolled across the floor. It pushed up against the sticky walls and rose above the bottom step of the staircase. It even trickled beneath the front door and out onto the street.

Otto looked over at Heinz and Helmut. They hadn't been quick enough to jump onto one of the tables, and their boots were now caked in paste. They were seething with rage.

"Otto!" they screamed. Their voices barreled up the rotting staircase, so even Frau Ferber could hear the commotion. "You're going to the cellar!"

Heinz pushed Otto down the cellar stairs. A second later, Helmut pulled him back out. Otto thought they'd changed their minds, but Helmut had other ideas.

"Shoes," he said.

"Huh?"

"Give me your shoes. You ruined mine, so now I get yours."

"But they won't fit," Otto said. His feet were a lot smaller than Helmut's.

"I don't care."

Before Helmut threw him to the ground and ripped the shoes off, Otto handed them over. It felt like everything he had owned when he lived in Dortzig was slowly being snatched away by the people of Hodeldorf. If he stayed much longer, he feared he wouldn't have anything left.

"Now get in."

This time when Heinz pushed Otto into the cellar, no one pulled him back out. The door closed behind him, and a key turned in the lock.

Otto was cast into darkness. Rats hissed and scampered around him. Otto's legs buckled. What if Klaus and Frida were wrong? What if they'd been mistaken? What if Elke and Nim were two different people? Was he about to be eaten alive?

A rat scampered over Otto's foot. He felt its claws latching on to his old socks. At least Helmut hadn't taken those too.

"Nibbles?" Otto whispered. "Is that you?" He reached down into the darkness, and his fingers closed around fur. The rat he touched wasn't wearing a coat. He quickly let it go.

Otto slowly climbed down the stairs. Rats kept scampering over his feet, but none tried to eat him. The dirt walls felt warm, like there was a sun in the ground heating them. If Otto weren't so scared, it would have been quite comfortable down there in the dark.

Otto wondered what he should do. The note said he had to go to the cellar. It didn't mention anything after that.

Otto waited in the warm cellar for what felt like hours. As the minutes passed, his fear grew. Nim wasn't coming to get him. It had been a trick. He was either going to wait in the cellar until he died of thirst and starvation, or eventually Helmut and Heinz would let him out. Then he'd have to face the wrath of Frau Ferber. He didn't know which was worse. He felt silly for trusting the note and sad that this was how it would end. He would never get the chance to find his mother. They would both die alone and lost in Hodeldorf.

At some point, Otto was pulled from his awful imaginings by the sound of something metal clanging to the ground.

"Who's there?" he said, panic flooding his body.

"It's Nim," came the hissed reply. "Come on. Let's go."

Otto felt a hand grab hold of his own and lead him through the darkness.

"You've got to crawl through here," Nim whispered. She had to keep her voice low, so that Helmut or Heinz wouldn't hear.

Otto ran his fingers along the warm dirt wall. He felt a gap just wide enough for him to fit through. He crawled down into the passage.

"How did you find this place?" Otto said as they crept through the tunnel.

"When I was sent down here, it had been raining for days. Water had started to fill the cellar. I thought I was going to drown. The rats did too. They were climbing all over me. But the water wasn't rising. I couldn't understand. It was still raining outside; I could hear it. The water was slowly draining out. That's when I found the grate. Someone must have installed it when the factory was built, to stop the cellar from flooding.

I don't think Frau Ferber knows it's there. I pulled off the cover and found this tunnel, and then I crawled out with the rats. When we got outside, most of the rats scampered off, but one of them stayed behind. Nibbles hasn't left me since. I think he wanted to escape the factory as much as I did."

Otto realized Nim was more than just a thief. She'd had a hard life—probably harder than he could even imagine. No wonder she had kept one of his coins. She'd had to fight to survive the factory, and she was still fighting to survive on the streets.

The passage led to a small alley that ran behind Frau Ferber's factory. Otto stepped out into the cold sun. The day had almost passed and was coming to an end. Nim started to place the metal grate over the passage they had escaped through.

"What are you doing?" Otto said.

"We need to cover it back up," Nim replied. "Otherwise, Frau Ferber might see."

"But what about the others? They're still trapped inside. Can't we help them too?"

"It's too risky," Nim said. "Frau Ferber won't miss one or two children. But if a whole bunch of them start to disappear, she'll know they aren't being eaten by rats. She'll send her sons out to fetch them back."

"Then we have to tell someone," Otto said. Bertha may not have told anyone about the conditions inside the factory, but he would. The adults would learn the truth and help set the children free. The city guards might even lock Frau Ferber up.

"It won't happen," Nim said.

"How do you know?" Otto asked. "You haven't even tried."

"Yes, I have!" Nim said. "When I escaped from the factory, I told everyone what it was like. I told the tattercoats. I told the storekeepers. I even told the city guards. And what did they do?"

Otto didn't know.

"They did nothing. They said I was just a silly little girl who didn't know what she was talking about. None of the adults in this city care about us. They see us tattercoats sleeping on the rooftops and starving in the streets every day, and none of them ever try to help. No one cares about the children in the factory. They only care about themselves."

"That's why we need to get them out," Otto said.

"I know," Nim agreed. "But I don't know how. Not yet. I've been thinking about it for years but still haven't been able to come up with a plan. Now come on." She closed the cover to the drain. "We need to get out of here before Frau Ferber sees."

They ran off down the lane. When the factory was out of sight, they came to a stop.

"What now?" Otto asked.

"Now I go back to my chimney."

"What about me?" Otto said. "What should I do?"

"That's up to you."

"But I have nowhere to go. I don't have any money either, and I still don't have a coat." The initial run from the factory had warmed Otto up. But now the heat was swiftly leaving, and the deep cold of Hodeldorf was creeping back in. It was rising through his old socks and leaching into his bones.

Nim wanted to keep walking, but something held her back. Otto still needed help. And if anyone in the city could help him survive on the streets, it would be a tattercoat like her.

"All right," Nim said. "You can come with us. But there are two conditions. Don't ever say I'm as bad as Blink again, and you have to be nice to Nibbles."

Chapter Fourteen

THE CODE OF THE TATTERCOATS

Now that Otto was free of Frau Ferber's factory, there was something important that had to be done.

"Let's get that black stuff off your hands," Nim said the morning after he'd escaped. They'd spent the night beside her chimney. With no coat to keep him warm, Otto had nestled between the bricks and Nim. It had kept the worst of the chill away, but he hadn't stopped shivering since he left the factory. In an attempt to keep warm, he jogged as they made their way to the main square.

"This is the place," Nim said when they arrived. They stood in front of a stall that sold all types of soap: sweet milk, dill, parsley, and holly.

"That's the one we want," Nim whispered, nodding to the box that held the holly soap. "It's the only thing in the whole city that'll get the muck off your hands. Trust me. I tried almost every soap in Hodeldorf, and it was the only one that worked."

Nim reached out to take the soap, but Otto pulled her back.

"You can't steal it," he whispered. "Stealing's wrong."

"Well, it's not like we can buy it. We don't have any money."

"Maybe we could ask for it," Otto said.

"You mean *beg*?" Nim couldn't believe what she was hearing. "There's no point begging 'round here. No one's going to give you anything for free. You've got two hands, Otto. They're not for holding out and asking people to fill them. They're for grabbing things: things you really need from people who have more than they should."

"But that's stealing, and I'm not a thief."

"Better a thief than a beggar," Nim said.

"No, it isn't," Otto replied.

"Well, I've lived on these streets for four years, and I've never met a single tattercoat who got anything from begging. Do you know why?"

Otto shook his head.

"Because if they'd spent all their time begging,

they'd be dead on account of not having any food to eat or a coat to keep them warm. Besides, the man who owns this stall is so rich he has two houses. A man with two houses won't miss a bar of soap."

Otto had to admit Nim had a point. He remained silent as she slipped the soap into her pocket. Then they made their way toward one of the public fountains in the main square.

"It'll take a long time to clean your hands," Nim said as they walked. "I reckon you'll need a good two hours at least to get that grime off."

"Two hours?" Otto asked.

"I wouldn't complain if I were you. I've spent four years trying to wash the grime off Nibbles, and it still won't come out. It's better than it was, though. He was black when we left the factory. Besides, it'll give me a chance to tell you about the code."

"What code?"

"The Tattercode. It's a set of rules all true tatter-coats must follow. If you're not going to be one of Frau Ferber's children, you're going to have to be one of us. No one survives for long on their own in Hodeldorf."

Otto didn't look too pleased about this. From the little he knew about tattercoats, he knew they liked to steal.

"You could leave, of course," Nim said. "Go some-place else."

"I can't leave without my mother."

"Then you'll need to be a tattercoat. Any boy or girl who has nowhere else to go can be one of us. But you've got to follow the rules. If people find out you've broken them, you're out. That's it. Well, you can break them a little," Nim conceded. "Once, Skid took more than he should have when a lady dropped her shopping. But Sage let him stay because he shared the food with Roe and promised never to do it again."

They reached the fountain. Otto wet his hands and began to lather them with soap. The water was slightly warm because the pipes were heated.

"The code has existed for as long as the tattercoats," Nim said. "That's longer than we've been alive. The Tattercode is made up of five rules. Rule one: when you become a tattercoat, you must choose your own name. It's a name that's made to match you. Take me, for example. I used to be called something else, but when I became a tattercoat I chose my *proper* name. The name that matched me like a coat that was measured and stitched to my exact size. I'm called Nim because I'm quick. Fast. Light on my feet. Nimble as a fox. My friend Skid chose his name because when he stole his first coat he skidded on the icy cobbles and almost broke his leg. And Blink chose his name because if you blink you'll miss him. He's the finest pickpocket I've ever known and he was the fastest tattercoat there ever was."

Otto tried to think of a name for himself but couldn't. He wasn't quick like Blink or nimble like Nim. He was just ordinary.

"Rule two," Nim continued. "If another tattercoat is in trouble, you must *always* help them out. After all, in Hodeldorf no one else is going to look out for us, so we've got to look after one another. As a tattercoat, you can never leave another tattercoat behind."

Otto liked the sound of that rule. It wasn't nice to be alone. It made him think of all the other children still trapped inside Frau Ferber's factory. He wished they had come with him to the cellar. Then they would all be free. He wondered if he would ever get the chance to save them. Maybe if he found his mother, she could help him get them out.

"Rule three," Nim said as Otto kept on lathering. "Tattercoats only ever steal what they need, and not a nickel or crust more. If we steal only a little bit, there'll be enough for everyone."

"That does make sense," Otto admitted.

"It also helps with rule four," Nim said. "A tattercoat must live without leaving a trail. You can't leave a trace of yourself anywhere."

"Why not?" Otto asked. He didn't like the sound of that rule. It sounded too much like what had happened to his mother. If she had left something behind, he might have been able to find her.

"Because it's dangerous. If I left my things on the Vidlers' roof, they'd know I was sleeping there and kick me off. Without a warm chimney to sleep beside, I'd freeze in the night. And if I left my things lying in the street, someone would steal them. Maybe not another tattercoat, but definitely a thief."

"About this thief-and-tattercoat thing," Otto said. He rinsed his hands under the water and lathered on more soap. "I still don't understand the difference."

"It all comes down to rule three," Nim said. "Thieves just steal whatever they want, but a tattercoat only steals when it's necessary. If a tattercoat saw a man eating two schnitzels for lunch, the tattercoat would steal one. That way, the man would still have lunch and someone else would too. If a thief saw that same man, he would take both schnitzels, all his money, his coat, and maybe even his shoes. By the time the thief was finished, the man would have lost his lunch, his clothing, and his dignity. A tattercoat would *never* rob anyone of that. We only take what we need in order to get by."

Otto had to admit he could see a difference between the two.

"What's the last rule?" he asked.

"It's the most important rule of all," Nim said. "It's the golden rule. The fifth rule is you can only ever own one coat at a time, and you can't get a new one until the old one becomes tatters."

"I wish I still had *my* coat," Otto said.

"Well, there's no point wishing it back now. Once Blink steals something, you'll never get it back. Besides, it'll just be a tatty coat one day. Might take longer than most because it's so fancy and all. But it'll happen. Everything 'round here turns to tatters," Nim said glumly.

Nim's glumness was contagious. It was hard for Otto to feel anything else now that he was stuck in a freezing city without a coat or a mother.

"Why does Blink have so many coats?" Otto asked.

"Because he's greedy," Nim said. "He's a thief. He used to only have one coat, like all of us, but then he stole a second and was thrown out."

"He must have been really cold," said Otto.

"Of course he was. Who isn't? But he didn't have to steal Snot's coat."

"Snot?" Otto said. He'd never heard that name before. "Who's Snot?"

"Snot was a tattercoat," Nim said sadly. "He chose his name on account of always having a runny nose. Snot and Blink were best friends. One night, during the worst coldstorm in ten years, Blink stole Snot's coat. While Blink slept with two coats, Snot had none. In the morning, Snot was dead. Sure, the cold killed him, but the cold only got to him because of Blink. Blink was greedy. Blink broke the code in more ways than one. Now he spends his days stealing coats he doesn't need and all sorts of other things as well."

Otto realized why Nim had been so upset when he compared her to Blink. He had been wrong. She wasn't anywhere near as bad as Blink. He bet if Blink had seen him in the factory he wouldn't have done anything to get him out.

"Now, come on." Nim nodded to Otto's hands. "Keep scrubbing. Once they're clean, they can be put to work."

"You don't mean stealing, do you?"

"Oh yes," Nim said with a glint in her eye. "And I know exactly what you need to steal first."

It took two hours for Nim to convince Otto to steal a coat. At first, he refused. He didn't want to steal anything from anyone. But the cold of Hodeldorf soon won out. He'd been spoiled by the warmth of the boot polish factory, and now the city felt even colder than when he'd first arrived.

"All right," he said. His hands were purple, and his arms were covered in goose bumps. He was cold in every bone of his body. "I'm ready."

Nim's eyes lit up. "About time. If you waited any longer, you might have frozen in the streets. Now, come on. Let's get to work."

Nim hauled Otto around the main square, pointing out various coats.

"What about that one? Or how about that?" she would say of the coats passing by. But no matter which coat Nim pointed to, Otto kept shaking his head.

"Fine," Nim eventually said after a whole hour of searching. "We'll look somewhere else."

Otto and Nim left the main square and went to Hodeldorf station. A train had just pulled in, and passengers were preparing to step on board.

"Do you see any you like?" Nim asked as they watched the people crossing the platform.

Otto didn't reply. Nim turned around. The boy was gone.

"Otto?" Nim hissed. She searched the platform. He was standing at the ticket counter.

Nim arrived just in time to hear Otto ask the stationmaster, "So you're certain she hasn't boarded a train?"

"Absolutely. I'd remember a coat like hers anywhere."

Otto sighed. "Okay. Thanks."

Nim pulled him away from the counter. "There'll be plenty of time to search for your mother. But right now we need to find you a coat." She spun Otto around so he was facing the passengers. "Come on, now. Are you sure you don't see any you like?" she repeated.

Otto shook his head. "None are as nice as my old one."

"Of course they aren't." Nim sighed. "You'd be searching for years to find another like that."

"Not if I get it back."

Nim sighed again. "I've already told you. Blink's too quick for us to snatch it off him."

"But what if it fell off and we were there to pick it up? Or we might find another coat lying about that no one wants."

Nim laughed. "In a city as cold as Hodeldorf, no one's going to hand you a coat. Now, come on. Choose one already. We're running out of options."

They had been standing on the platform for so long half the passengers had left. Another train wasn't due until tomorrow.

"You've got to be smart about this," Nim whispered. "You need it to be big enough to grow into and thick enough to keep you warm."

"Okay," Otto said. "But wha—"

"I've found it," Nim said, cutting Otto off. "I've found the perfect one."

Otto followed her gaze. A man stood by the ticket counter. Two thick leather suitcases rested beside his feet. He was wearing one coat, and another—a heavy one colored deep blue—lay on top of the suitcases.

"Now's your chance," Nim said. "You won't get another like this. I bet he owns heaps of coats."

Otto didn't move.

"Go on," Nim said. "I'm not stealing it for you. Look. I'll distract him, and you take the coat."

Before Otto could argue, Nim darted across the platform. True to her name, she was nimble as a fox. She grabbed one of the suitcases and disappeared into the crowd.

"Give that back!" the man with two coats screamed. "Hand it over, you little thief!" He took off after Nim.

This was Otto's chance. While everyone on the platform watched Nim, he ran over to the forgotten suitcase. He reached out and touched the coat draped on top. The coat wasn't very soft, but it was thick, and he figured it would keep him warm.

"Go on," a person hissed. Nim had doubled back and now stood beside him. "What are you waiting for? This is the easiest steal you'll ever get."

Before he came to Hodeldorf, Otto never imagined he would ever steal anything. But the cold of the city was eating into his bones, and he knew Nim was right: no one was going to give him a coat for free. So he reached out and snatched it.

Unfortunately, the stationmaster saw what was happening and blew his whistle. Nim and Otto didn't wait around. In a flash, they were off. They stopped running only when the station was far behind them, and it was clear no one had followed. Otto's feet had been cut by the cobbles, but they were so cold he couldn't feel any pain.

"Go on." Nim nodded to the coat. "Put it on."

With heavy hands, Otto put on the equally heavy coat. As soon as the cloth settled over his shoulders, he felt warm for the first time since leaving Frau Ferber's factory.

"Don't worry, Otto," Nim said. She placed a supportive hand on the sleeve of his new coat. "You're no thief. You're a tattercoat, and there's no shame in being one of us."

At the same moment Otto was putting on his new coat, two boys were opening the door to Frau Ferber's cellar. It was almost time for the daily counting, and they knew Otto would not be passing it.

"Wakey, wakey," Helmut said as he peered down into the darkness. Silence greeted him.

"Get up," Heinz ordered.

Nothing stirred inside the cellar. Even the rats were quiet.

"You better go and check on him," Heinz said.

"Me?" Helmut asked. "I'm not going down there."

"Well, I'm not going either."

In the end, they sent Frida in. After searching every corner of the cellar, she failed to find any trace of Otto.

"It's like he's disappeared," Frida said as she climbed back up the stairs.

"But he can't have," Helmut hissed. "The door's been locked the whole time."

"He must have been eaten by the rats," Heinz said. "They even ate all his clothes. There's not a trace of him left."

Chapter Fifteen

THE WELCOMING CEREMONY

That night, a ceremony was held in the streets of Hodeldorf. The clanging of metal garbage lids called the tattercoats together. They gathered in a small alley near the main square.

The tattercoats lined both sides of the alley. They held small glass jars full of twigs. They'd lit the twigs, and now little smoky dragons, fiery giants, and evil crows flew around inside the old glass. They threw their shadows upon the walls of the alley, so it looked like real beasts and monsters were circling about.

"The twigs were gathered from Hodeldorf Wood," one of the tattercoats whispered to Otto. "The wood-cutters bring them back with the wood. They're magical, like the forest itself."

Nim snorted. "They're not magical," she whispered to Otto. "It's a trick. I don't know how Sage does it. But I do know this. Magic isn't real. It's just not possible."

Otto stared at the shadows flickering in the night. He had never seen such wondrous beasts. He trusted Nim, but he didn't trust her on this. How could Sage be creating these creatures? It looked like magic to him. He had a feeling the woods around the city held all sorts of things. He also had a feeling that when he'd caught the train into the city, there truly had been creatures watching him. It wasn't just his imagination.

"Tonight, we welcome a new tattercoat into our group," said Sage. "He has taken his first step down the tattercoat path. He has stolen his first coat. May it keep him warm and safe until it turns to tatters. Welcome, Otto," Sage said. She motioned for Otto to approach.

Otto walked down the shining alley. Nim remained at the back, holding a glass jar of her own. Nibbles was sitting on top of it, watching the ceremony intently. The little flames burning inside warmed his bottom half rather nicely. When Otto reached the end of the alley, he stopped before Sage, who recited the Tattercode. When she had voiced the final rule, she looked down at Otto and said, "Do you swear to live by the Tattercode?"

"I do," Otto said.

"And do you swear to live by this code until you are a grown-up?"

Otto paused. He wanted to say yes, but he knew it would be a lie. So he told the truth.

"I swear to live by this code until I find my mother."

A nervous ripple of whispers passed among the crowd. Sage looked unsure for a moment, but then nodded her head.

"I accept that as your oath," she said. "If any of us was granted the chance to be with our own mother or father, we would take it. Now, what is your tattercoat name?"

Otto paused. He hadn't thought about this. He tried to think about it now but couldn't come up with any name that fit.

"Can I just be Otto?" he asked.

Another round of whispers passed among the group. A few of the tattercoats lining the path shook their heads. Even Sage looked upset by this. She frowned and thought for some time. Then she spoke.

"The code states you must choose your own name when you join the tattercoats. If you choose your old name, that is still a choice. You can remain as Otto. Welcome, Otto Tattercoat."

Sage motioned for Otto to turn around. The closest tattercoat in the procession stepped forward.

"My name is Tricky Tattercoat," she said. "I welcome you, Otto Tattercoat, and gift you with a glass jar of your own. A glass jar you can use for storing things." She handed Otto an empty jar and then stepped back into the line.

The next tattercoat stepped forward. He introduced himself as Slink and gifted Otto a piece of stolen rope for tying things together.

The next tattercoat was Roe. She introduced herself and gifted him a pair of shoes.

"They're very old and smell very bad, but they should stop your toes from turning black and falling off. I stole them from a dead man. I'm not sure if they'll fit."

One by one, the tattercoats stepped forward and introduced themselves, then gifted Otto something they had stolen just for him. Even though Otto didn't agree with stealing, he was very glad to have a few things to help him survive on the streets.

Nim was the last tattercoat to step forward. Her arms were empty, and she did not need to introduce herself. She also did not give Otto a gift he could touch. Instead, her gift was a promise.

"I promise to help you search for your mother. I will ask about her in the streets. I will call out her name from the rooftops. I will sneak into houses purely for the purpose of seeing if your mother is inside, and not for stealing, not even things I really need. This is my gift to you, Otto Tattercoat."

"Thank you," Otto said. It was, out of every gift he'd received that night, the best gift of all.

Nim stepped back into line. The tattercoats unscrewed the lids of their jars, and the flaming smoke trapped inside danced up into the night. All around them, the air filled with smoke. Clouds that looked like elves and wolves and flying horses swirled through the alley. The smoke rose higher before dispersing into nothing.

The alley grew dark, and the tattercoats dispersed too. Now there was one extra among them. A boy in a scratchy navy coat, called Otto.

As Otto was welcomed into the tattercoats, another boy mourned being expelled.

Blink had heard the clanging of the bins—the traditional call to gather—and he'd followed the sound to the alley. Afraid of being seen, he'd remained hidden in the shadows.

The last welcoming ceremony Blink had attended was for his best friend. On that night, the newly orphaned Friedrich had chosen his new name: Snot. Afterward, Blink had given him a handkerchief to wipe his runny nose. Blink had the handkerchief now. It had been in Snot's coat pocket when Blink had taken it.

To keep his mind off Snot and the terrible end he'd suffered, Blink focused on the ceremony. At first, he hadn't recognized the boy being welcomed. But as Nim made him a promise, he realized who it was. The boy who used to wear a green coat now wore one of blue. It wasn't as nice as his old one. But even though Blink was wearing the finest coat in the city, and seven more underneath, he would have given them all away if it meant he could rejoin the tattercoats.

Unfortunately, Blink knew that would never happen. Along with the five spoken rules of the Tattercode, there was a sixth rule that remained unspoken—the rule that said once a tattercoat was expelled from the group, they could never, ever return.

Chapter Sixteen

A TALK OF MOTHERS

True to her word, Nim did everything she could to help Otto find his mother. The day after the welcoming ceremony, she set off from her chimney and, instead of robbing people, asked them a question. For the entire day, the streets of the city rang out with the same five words: "Have you seen Marta Schneider?"

Unfortunately for Otto, those five words were always followed with the same answer: "No."

When no one could tell her where Otto's mother was, Nim began to look for her instead. With the help of the other tattercoats, she searched every shop in the city along with every home. To make sure they didn't miss any, Sage drew a map of the city and allocated two streets to each tattercoat. The tattercoats could be very organized when they needed to be. But no matter where they looked, they came up empty-handed. There was no trace of Otto's mother anywhere.

"I'm sorry," Roe said to Otto. They were sitting in the main square with Nim and Skid. All four were searching for their dinner.

"That's okay," Otto said. "You tried your best."

"What was she like?" Skid asked. "Your mother," he clarified. "I never had one."

"She was wonderful," Otto said. "She was the finest seamstress in all of Dortzig. People would order clothes one year in advance, because she was so busy. But even when she was busy, she always made time for me. We'd go for walks together, she'd make delicious stews and strudels, and at night she'd run me a bath."

"That's awful," Nim said. "I hate baths. At Frau Ferber's, she made us take one bath a year, and we all had to use the same water. By the time the second person climbed in, it was like you were swimming in the vat of boot polish."

"Well, my mother's baths were nothing like that. She used to make me the most wonderful baths. She'd fill the tub with steaming-hot water, and herbs she found in the woods. After one of her baths, I'd smell fresh for days."

"I don't know if my mother ever gave me a bath," Nim said. "But she did wrap her coat around me once. I know, because that's how they found me."

"My mother wasn't like either of yours," Roe said sadly. "She spent our money on a special drink she would have all the time. Once, I went a whole week without food, even though she never went a day without her drink. Eventually, she said I was costing her too much money, so she tried to hand me to Frau Ferber. But I had an inkling she was bad. So, as my mother let go of me and Frau Ferber reached out, I ran away as quick as I could. That's how I became a tattercoat."

As he listened to the tattercoats talk, Otto realized that even though he'd lost his mother, he was still one of the lucky ones. He couldn't imagine his mother giving him away or choosing a special drink over him. Realizing how lucky he was to have such a wonderful mother made him even more desperate to find her.

"I hope you find her," Skid said to Otto, almost like he could hear his thoughts. "It's nice to have a mother, even a nasty one like Roe's."

"You know what I'd also love?" Nim said.

The other children shook their heads.

"I'd love my very own bedroom. It wouldn't have to be big," Nim said. "But big enough for me and Nibbles. There'd be a bed with a thick red blanket; shelves full of books so I wouldn't have to wait for Sage to tell me a story, I could just choose one for myself; and a fireplace that was always burning so the cold would never creep in."

"Would I be able to visit?" Roe asked.

"Of course," Nim said. "All my friends could come."

The four of them sat in silence, imagining their own dream bedrooms, until they saw half a schnitzel fall onto the ground.

"Quick," Nim yelled. "Before someone else snatches it."

The lights shone on the top floor of the boot polish factory. The streets outside were dark. The tattercoats were all asleep on the rooftops, nestled against their warm chimneys. But Frau Ferber remained awake, sitting in her study.

Frau Ferber often had trouble sleeping. It was her thoughts that kept her awake. Sometimes she thought about the children sleeping on the floor below. They were an awfully ungrateful lot. Without her, they'd be living alone on the streets. They'd either starve to death or freeze in their sleep. She was their savior. They should have been paying her.

Sometimes Frau Ferber thought about her sons. They weren't the brightest pair, but they were hers, so she had to keep them. Besides, they worked for free as well, and they were as loyal as they came. She knew she could trust them to keep the factory running smoothly, because they stood to inherit it.

But mostly Frau Ferber thought about her mother.

Frau Ferber had been her mother's only child. She'd never known her father. Her mother said that was because her father didn't want to know her. Sometimes Frau Ferber used to think her mother didn't want to know her either.

Frau Ferber's mother had inherited the boot polish factory from her own father. Back then, adults had worked to fill the jars of blacking paste. It wasn't until twenty years ago that Frau Ferber had the idea of getting children to work in the factory. That way, she could make the jars smaller but still sell them for the same price, and the children could work for free. This decision had made her very rich.

But even with all the money she had stashed away in her office and in a vault at the city bank, she felt like a failure. For years she couldn't understand why. Then, one night about five years ago, it had clicked.

When she was younger, her mother always used to moan about how she didn't want to pass the factory on to her.

"You'll ruin all my good work, Flora," she would say. "You don't know anything about quotas or capital or profits or business. This factory will be closed within a week of you taking over."

No matter how hard Frau Ferber had tried to show her mother she could do it—she started working on the factory floor when she was eight and knew every factory worker's name by nine—her mother still believed she would fail.

All the changes she had made to the factory— bringing the children in, increasing the quotas and decreasing the food—had made the profits soar. But even though Frau Ferber knew this, her mother never could. She had died long before the changes were made.

Frau Ferber wished her mother could come back to life, even just for a day, to see all the work she had done. She knew that if she could see the figures in the books, see the money in the bank, and see the number of boot polish jars hurtling off across the country by train, she would realize she had been wrong about her daughter. Flora wasn't stupid or worthless. She was smart and ruthless, and in her hands the factory had become the most profitable business in all of Hodeldorf.

One day, she'd open up another factory, and perhaps even another. She'd snatch all the children off the streets, and perhaps a few from their homes as well. Her profits would triple! She wouldn't just be the richest person in Hodeldorf; she'd be the richest person in the country.

Chapter Seventeen

THE THREE TOLLS

After the failed search to find Otto's mother, the days in Hodeldorf grew colder and shorter than usual. One morning, it was so cold Nim and Otto didn't climb down from the roof at dawn. By the time midday came, they were still huddled against the chimney. The air was so frosty even Nibbles's whiskers had an icy lace to them.

"I didn't think anyplace could be this cold," Otto said through chattering teeth. He was now very glad he'd stolen a coat. If he hadn't, he bet he would have frozen during his sleep.

The entire city seemed to have come to a stop. It was even too cold to snow. But that didn't mean there was no snow around: in fact, the snow that had fallen one week before was now frozen solid. If you tried to walk in the streets, you almost always slipped. Soon, even the smoke that rose from the chimneys froze and clattered down onto the rooftops.

"This isn't just a cold snap," Nim said that night as she huddled close to the chimney with Otto and Nibbles. "This feels like a true coldstorm. The kind of storm where people die. The kind of storm that killed my parents—and Snot."

The following day, Nim's fears were confirmed. The clock-tower bells tolled three times at dawn. It was now officially a coldstorm. When they braved the main square in search of food, they learned a tattercoat had died in the night.

"Tricky died in her sleep," Skid said. "Frozen solid against the Wagners' chimney. The fire went out during the night, and none of the Wagners relit it. Two of them died too."

The cold was showing no signs of going away. Nim knew things would only get worse. She also knew the tattercoats were at the greatest risk of dying in the cold. It was always those living on the streets who succumbed first. They needed somewhere warm to stay, and, after saving Otto, Nim knew just the place. But there was a problem. Most of the tattercoats would prefer to freeze in the streets rather than go there.

• • •

"It's the only place we can stay warm," Nim said to the tattercoats gathered before her. The clanging of garbage lids had called them to the same alley where Otto was welcomed into the group.

"There's no way we're going there," one of the tattercoats yelled.

"Yeah," yelled a few of the others. "We're not going into Frau Ferber's factory!"

Ever since Nim had escaped from Frau Ferber's, she'd blocked all memories of that place. Rescuing Otto had reminded her that there was one good thing about the factory. It was warm, and if they could make use of that warmth without being caught, maybe they would all survive this coldstorm.

"But I'm not asking you to go *into* Frau Ferber's factory," she said. "I'm asking you to go *under* it. The cellar is warm. I don't know why, but it is. It's the warmest place in the whole city. If we sleep in there, there's no chance we'll freeze."

"But we might get caught," Skid said. "And then we'll be locked in the factory forever."

"We won't get caught. Not if we're quiet. Frau Ferber never goes into the cellar. Even Heinz and Helmut are too frightened to step inside. And all the other children are too. Apart from Otto, no one's been in that cellar for four years."

Nim had hoped her words would convince the

other tattercoats that the cellar was the safest place they could be. But none looked convinced.

"Fine," Nim said. "I can't force you to do anything. But if anyone wants to sleep in the warmth tonight, you can meet me and Otto on the corner of Sonne Street just before dusk."

Otto and Nim stood on the street corner and waited. "I don't think anyone's coming," Otto said to Nim. They stood one street away from Frau Ferber's cellar. From this angle, they couldn't be seen through any windows of the factory.

"They still have a few minutes," Nim said.

The city grew dark. Nim feared no one else would show. Then a cluster of children appeared at the end of the street. As they got closer, Nim made out the shapes of Skid and Roe. More than ten other tattercoats followed. Half of the group had come.

The tattercoats waited until it was truly dark. Then Nim raced over to the factory and opened the grate. One by one, the tattercoats sneaked into the cellar. Nim was the last one inside and closed the grate behind her. If anyone walked past during the night, they would have no idea that a group of tattercoats slept on the other side. Hopefully, Frau Ferber wouldn't either.

Chapter Eighteen

THE BLIND GIANT

Word quickly spread that the cellar below Frau Ferber's factory truly was as warm as Nim had said. With each passing night, the number of tattercoats seeking refuge grew. Soon, all the tattercoats lined up outside at night to get inside— even Sage. As the days grew colder, the tattercoats spent more time inside the cellar than out. Soon, they left only for a few hours during the day, to stretch their legs and steal food.

One day, Nim went out to steal some dinner. Dusk was falling over the icy city. Fires burned inside the homes she passed, and chugged smoke into the darkening sky. Most people in Hodeldorf remained inside.

The woodcutters were the only people spending

more time outside than in. They were constantly leaving the city gates to fell wood, cut it, and haul it back to the city. It was a dangerous job, but it had to be done. If the city ran out of wood, the fires would go out, and all the city folk would freeze in their sleep.

The main square was almost empty when Nim arrived. Fewer than half the stalls were open, and only a few customers passed between them.

The lack of crowds made Nim stand out. Every time she neared a stall, the owners scowled and moved their wares away. It was getting more difficult to steal: all the tattercoats were having trouble. In desperation, Sage had broken into the home of a wealthy duke and stolen enough to feed everyone. But when she'd gone back to steal more the following week, she had found the house bolted up, and even the windows had bars on them.

Nim was starting to fear she would go without dinner when she noticed a trail of food on the cobbles. She followed the food with her eyes. It led to a woman whose grocery bag had split. Nim scooped up the items.

"Excuse me," she called.

The woman turned and scowled.

"What do you want?" she said. She didn't like talking to tattercoats. She didn't even like looking at them.

"You dropped these." Nim held out the groceries. "There's a hole in your bag."

"Oh." The woman stopped scowling. "Thank you." She took the food from Nim and hurried down the road.

"She could have at least given me something in thanks," Nim mumbled to Nibbles. "Or invited me to sleep in front of her fire for the night."

Luckily, Nim had expected her not to and had kept a little treat for herself. She reached beneath her coat and pulled out a large sausage, which she'd stuck under her stockings. "There's enough here to share with everyone."

Nibbles had followed the sausage out from beneath Nim's coat. He twitched his whiskers and licked his lips. He loved sausage.

"All right," Nim said. "You can have a little bit now." She peeled back the oiled paper that protected the meat and tore off a piece. Nibbles gobbled it right up.

Nim was just tearing off some for herself when someone tried to snatch the whole sausage.

"Hey!" she shouted. "Get off, Blink." She pushed his hand away. Instead of trying to grab the sausage again, he looked down at the ground.

"Please, Nim," he said. "Can I have a piece? It doesn't have to be big. I just need something. I haven't eaten for days."

Nim would have thought it was a trick, only she could tell it wasn't. Beneath his bright green coat, Blink looked pale and thin. The eight coats he wore swamped his small frame. His legs were so weak he could barely stand.

"Fine. Here you go." Nim gave Blink the piece of sausage meant for herself.

Blink stuffed the sausage in his mouth and chewed slowly.

"Thank you," he said. Instead of asking for more, he turned and walked away. He was almost gone when Nim called him back.

"Wait! Where are you going?"

"To my chimney."

Nim had no idea where Blink's chimney was, but she feared no chimney in the city would be warm enough to keep him alive. Not when he was this weak. Even though she was angry that Blink had stolen Snot's coat and then Otto's, Nim couldn't let him die for it.

"Come on." She nodded toward the opposite end of the square. "You can stay with us tonight."

"'Us'? You mean, with the tattercoats?" Blink said.

Nim nodded. "We've got a warm place to stay. You won't be cold in there."

When Blink reached the secret entrance to Frau Ferber's cellar, he didn't seem to realize where they were. He just followed Nim inside. When he emerged from the tunnel, it took several minutes for the other tattercoats to notice him in the dimly lit space. When they did, they were not pleased.

"Look, it's Blink," someone hissed.

"What's he doing here?" hissed a few more.

"Look," Nim said as loud as she dared. "None of us like Blink, not after what he did to Snot. But we can't just leave him out in the cold to die."

"Yes, we can," one of the tattercoats said. "That's what he did to Snot."

Some of the tattercoats pushed Blink back toward the tunnel. Nim stepped between them.

"Let him stay," she said, "or you won't get any of this." She reached into her pocket and pulled out the remaining sausage.

The smell of fatty and herby meat filled the cellar. The tattercoats fell silent as Nim broke the food apart. They were quiet as they ate, but once the food was gone, they began to argue again. Eventually, Sage grew tired of the disagreements and cut them off.

"Blink isn't a tattercoat anymore," Sage said, "but he's still a boy who needs somewhere safe to stay during the coldstorm. We've all lost someone in one of those."

Nim bowed her head. She had lost two.

"Now, everyone lie down and tuck your coats around you. I'll tell you a story to help you sleep."

At the offer of a story, the tattercoats quickly settled. Besides, none of them truly wanted Blink to die in the cold. They were just angry with him, and that made them say and do things they didn't really mean.

When all the tattercoats had fallen silent, Sage began her story. During a coldstorm, she knew exactly which one to tell.

Once there lived seven giants who were taller than the tallest tree in Hodeldorf Wood. But even though they were far taller than the tallest man, they were still children, and like all good children they did as their parents bid. Well, at least they tried to.

"You are free to roam all through these woods," their father told them on their fifth birthday, "but don't ever roam into the city. The people who live there fear things they don't understand, and they might hurt you."

The seven little giants listened to their father and never left the edge of the woods.

On their sixth birthday, their mother issued a new warning. "You are free to roam all through these woods, but don't ever roam into a witch's den. Though the witches are smaller than you, they are far more powerful."

The seven little giants listened to their mother and never ventured into a witch's den, no matter how welcoming it looked.

Their seventh birthday came, and their father said, "You are free to look at all the trees and the creatures in these woods, but don't ever look at the sun. The sun is so bright that if you look at it for even just a moment you will be blinded forever."

For several months, the seven giants did as they were told. But as their eighth birthday neared, one of them grew curious. It wasn't enough to see the trees around him or the ground beneath his feet. He wanted to see what was above. So one day while his brothers and sisters were playing in the woods, he walked to a space between the trees where the light from the sun filtered through. He stood in the warm rays and looked up.

True to his father's warning, when the little giant looked at the sun, the light was so bright it blinded him. For the rest of his life—three hundred years—he never saw anything again. But despite living in darkness for three centuries, he didn't regret looking at the sun because when he had, he'd seen something wonderful.

When the giant had looked up into the sky, he had seen a group of creatures—like jeweled snakes—flying through the air and breathing fire into the sun. No one had ever been brave enough

*to look at the sun before, so he was the first to
see the creatures. As the first to spot them, the
giant had the honor of naming them. He called
the creatures sundragons, because they made the
world warm and bright.*

*Years after the blind giant died, the world
started to grow cold and dark. The light of the
sun grew weak. Soon, giants and people could
look up without going blind, and when they did,
they saw only the sky. Either the blind giant had
lied or the sundragons had disappeared.*

"But I'll tell you this," Sage said to all the children
gathered in the cellar. "If we could find a sundragon—
even one—I bet this coldstorm would pass and the city
of Hodeldorf would grow warm once more."

As much as Nim wanted to believe the story, she
knew it wasn't true. Hodeldorf had been cold since she
was born, and it would be cold until she died. There
was no magical creature that was going to save the city.
They would have to save themselves.

That night, as they slept in the unusual warmth of Frau
Ferber's cellar, the usual dreams of the tattercoats were
interrupted. Instead of Nim dreaming of her lost parents, Otto dreaming of finding his mother, and Roe

dreaming that her own mother had chosen her over her special drink, they all dreamed the same thing. They dreamed that in the morning when they awoke and stepped out into the cold, a sundragon soared past and made the world warm. It grew so hot they took off their tatty coats and never had to wear them again.

Chapter Nineteen

A LEAD

"I think the cold's easing off," Frau Ferber said as she stared out the window of her study. It was early in the morning, and the sun was just rising over the city. The coldstorm had lain like a curse over Hodeldorf for two weeks. Now some of the chill had left. "Tell me again what you heard."

"Some of the children were talking again last night," Helmut said. "They were saying Otto wasn't eaten by rats. They said he escaped."

"Well, he can't have. No one escapes my factory."

"It *is* a bit strange the rats ate even his clothes," Heinz mused.

"What are you trying to say?" his mother asked.

Heinz wished he hadn't said anything, but realized his mother would be even more angry if he didn't answer her question. "Just that they might be right."

Frau Ferber thought for several moments. "I don't want the children thinking he escaped. We can't have their little minds filling with hope. We have to quash it down, or they'll try to escape too. We'll have a mutiny on our hands."

Heinz and Helmut nodded.

"No more sending them to the cellar as punishment," Frau Ferber said. "Fetch extra locks for the doors, and bars for the windows, and increase the daily quota to three hundred and fifty. We'll reduce their dinners by half as well. If we punish them enough, their hope will disappear, and they'll just focus on filling the jars."

Frau Ferber smiled at the thought of the money she would save on food. Her smile fell away when she noticed a child darting down the alley below.

"That's not one of our children, is it?" she asked her sons.

Heinz and Helmut hurried over to the window.

"I don't think so," Heinz said.

"Where did he come from?" Frau Ferber asked. The only building in the alley was the back end of her factory.

In answer to her question, a second child appeared in the alley. He had just climbed out of the brick wall below. He looked left and then right before darting after the first child.

"That's near the cellar," Frau Ferber said. "Perhaps the rats didn't get Otto after all." She looked at the child who had just sneaked out. "Do you recognize him?"

Her sons squinted at the boy running down the alley. He was wearing a navy coat.

"That's Otto," Helmut said.

"The children were right. The rats didn't get him after all." Frau Ferber let out a low growl. Another child emerged from her factory. It was a girl in a gray coat.

"She looks familiar," Frau Ferber said. "She must have escaped years ago. She probably helped the boy escape too."

"Should we go and get them?" Heinz asked.

Frau Ferber wanted to snatch the lot of them up and lock them in her factory. That would teach them a lesson. But she knew now wasn't the time. "It's too bright. It'll be easier to snatch them if we wait until it's dark."

Unaware they were being watched from above, Nim and Otto planned their day. With the coldstorm lifting, they could soon return to their chimney. Most of the tattercoats had already left, but a few were making the most of the warmth and planned to stay a little longer.

"Let's get some practice in," Nim said to Otto as they left the factory. "When I'm finished with you, you'll be the best tattercoat in all of Hodeldorf."

Despite Nim's high hopes, Otto quickly proved her wrong. Forget the best tattercoat in Hodeldorf. Otto was the worst. He spent the first hour complaining about how he didn't want to steal anything. Then, when he finally agreed to do so, he was caught before he'd taken anything. He'd looked at the storekeeper with so much guilt the man knew exactly what Otto was up to. He whacked him out of the store with the hard end of a broom.

When Otto tried to steal from someone's pocket, he didn't have much luck either. He grabbed the woman's leg instead, and the lady beat him away as well. At the end of four hours, he was bruised and battered and had yet to steal a thing.

Nim sighed and shook her head. "Let Nibbles show you how it's done."

Nim whistled, and Nibbles took off. He dove into a woman's bag and a moment later returned with two nickels tucked under his furry arm.

"See?" Nim said. In less than a minute, Nibbles had stolen more than Otto had managed in weeks. "Now"—Nibbles handed Nim the coins—"what should we have for dinner?"

They used the money to buy three bowls of pork knuckle soup. They were just slurping up the broth when another tattercoat raced over.

"Otto," Skid said. He was out of breath but didn't

stop to catch it. "I think I've found someone who saw your mother."

"It would have been almost three months ago," the man said. He was a woodcutter. "I was coming back from cutting wood in the forest when she was heading out. Had on a fine red coat, if I remember correctly, and carried a basket made of elm. Said her name was Marta."

"That's her!" Otto said. "She wove the basket herself. What did she say?"

"I asked where she was going. It's not every day you see a lady heading out into the forest alone, and when there's a full moon and all. She said she was going to collect herbs for her son. I warned her not to go. I said the woods around Hodeldorf are dangerous: things happen in there, things that can't happen anywhere else. But she didn't listen."

"What kind of things?" Otto asked.

"There are things in those woods that don't live anywhere else. Creatures who look like you and me but aren't like us at all. They play tricks with your mind and make you do things you don't want to do. Things like wolves who are as smart as humans, and music that forces you to follow it wherever it leads."

"But they're not real," Otto said. "They're just

stories, aren't they?" If things like that really did exist, his mother was in a lot of trouble.

"Something was real enough to take my father," the woodcutter said. "Fifty years ago, he and seven other woodcutters went missing in the woods and were never seen again. Half the city went in search of them. A suspect was eventually found. He was caged and led back through the trees. But before they reached the city, he escaped. Rumor is, someone let him go. Some believe he's still out in the woods today. Whatever happened, I don't want it to happen to me. That's why we woodcutters only chop trees on the edge of the forest. If we went in any deeper, we might never come back out."

For the first time in a long time, Otto shivered from something other than the cold.

"I think this could be good," Otto said that evening as he and Nim walked back to the factory.

"*Good?*" Nim couldn't believe what she was hearing. "Did you hear anything the woodcutter said?"

"Well, it's not good that all those awful things have happened. But this is why we couldn't find her. We've been looking in the wrong place. She isn't in the city. She's out there."

Otto pointed past the city walls to the thick woods

that rose beyond. The trees stood like giant sentinels against the darkening sky.

"We have to go there," he said. "We have to go in and find her."

"But we can't. You heard what the woodcutter said. The woods are dangerous. When people go in there, they disappear and never come out."

"But we have to. My mother is clearly in trouble. She would never just leave me—something must have happened, and now she can't get back. I have to find her and help her."

Nim sighed and shook her head.

"No one could have survived the coldstorm in the woods. If your mother was in there, she would have died from the cold, just like my parents. I'm sorry, Otto. If your mother went into those woods, she isn't ever coming out."

Otto was worried Nim was right. But even though he feared the worst, he still hoped for the best. It was like Skid said: he was lucky to have a mother. He needed to do everything he could to get her back. If Nim wasn't going to help him, he'd have to do it by himself.

Otto stopped walking and turned around.

"What are you doing?" Nim asked.

"Going to the woods."

"Don't be silly," Nim said. "You'll never survive out there."

"But I've got to try," Otto said. "I have to try and find her. Will you come with me?"

Nim looked at the giant trees that filled Hodeldorf Wood. A shiver raced down her spine. She was scared: more scared of the woods than anything—even Frau Ferber's factory. She had never left the city before.

"I'm sorry, Otto. I can't."

"Fine. I'll do it myself."

Otto turned from Nim and ran off into the darkening night. Within seconds, he was gone.

"I'm sure he'll be back tonight," Nim said to Nibbles as they hurried through the streets of the city. It felt a lot less safe when they were walking alone. "He'll realize it was a bad idea and turn around."

The lights of the boot polish factory appeared up ahead. Nim turned into the alley that led to the cellar. She was so focused on Otto that she failed to see two boys standing in the shadows. She was just kneeling to open the grate when someone grabbed her from behind.

Chapter Twenty

TWO TRUE TATTERCOATS

When Nim was first grabbed and then knocked to the ground, she thought she was being robbed. But when she saw the faces of the two boys behind her, she realized something far worse was about to happen.

"Leave me alone!" Nim yelled as Heinz leaned down and grabbed her arm.

Nibbles raced out of Nim's pocket and bit the boy's hand.

Heinz whacked his truncheon down, but Nibbles was quick; he'd already scampered away. Instead of hitting the dirty rat, he pounded his own fingers. A new wave of yells joined Nim's.

As Heinz nursed his bruised hand, Helmut made a grab for Nim. Nibbles jumped onto his arm and scurried onto his face. He clawed at Helmut's eyes. The boy threw Nibbles to the ground.

"Stop your whining," Helmut growled to Heinz, "and help me grab her."

Heinz slipped his truncheon into his belt and grabbed hold of Nim's legs. Helmut grabbed her by the arms and lifted her into the air. Nim kicked and screamed, but it was useless. She couldn't break free, and Nibbles was now too injured to help.

Nim was hauled down the lane. When they reached the corner, the front door of the boot polish factory came into sight. Nim knew she couldn't go back. If she did, she would never get out. They must have found out about the entrance to the cellar; there was no other way to escape.

"Please," she begged. "Just let me go. I'll do anything not to go back."

Helmut and Heinz laughed.

"You can't do anything for us," they said.

When her words failed to work, Nim tried to kick and punch the boys instead.

"Grab your truncheon," Helmut said to Heinz, "and give her a good whack."

Heinz let go of Nim and reached for his truncheon. But it wasn't there.

"I must have dropped it," he said.

A moment later, the truncheon whacked him on the head.

Heinz dropped to the ground like a sack of potatoes. A boy stood behind him.

"Blink?" Nim said.

In a flash, Blink whacked Helmut behind the knees. The older boy dropped Nim and fell to the ground.

"Come on!" Blink said.

"What about Nibbles?" said Nim. She had left him lying in the alley.

"Already got him." Blink reached into the pocket of Otto's stolen coat and pulled out a very stunned and confused rat. "Now hurry. We don't want those two catching up."

He grabbed Nim, and together they raced off into the night. They were several blocks away when Nim pulled Blink to a stop.

"We've got to go back," she said, panic rising in her voice. "What if they snatched the others?"

"What others?" Blink asked.

"Skid and Roe." They were the only other tatter-coats who had planned to go back to the cellar tonight. The rest had returned to their chimneys. "Come on."

Nim dragged Blink back to the factory. They stayed in the shadows as they edged toward the alley. By the light trickling down from Frau Ferber's study, they could see the lane was empty.

"Maybe they made it into the cellar," Nim whispered.

Though she was scared, Nim knew what she had to do. With a quick glance up at the windows of the factory—no people appeared to be watching—she raced back down the lane. She pulled on the grate. It didn't move. She pulled again. The grate had been glued shut. If Skid and Roe were in the cellar, they wouldn't be able to get back out.

Nim ran back to Blink. She was just about to tell him the bad news when Blink cut her off. He didn't have to say anything. He just pointed up.

Nim turned around and looked at Frau Ferber's factory. The window of the study wasn't empty anymore. They could see four people standing behind the glass: Heinz, Helmut, and two children in tatty coats. One coat was far too large, and the other was covered in faded suns. Skid and Roe had been snatched.

"We've got to do something," Nim said. "We have to save them." This was all her fault. If she hadn't convinced them to stay in the cellar, they never would have been caught.

"We can't do anything about it tonight," Blink said. "They'll be on the lookout. We'll come back later. I promise."

They left the boot polish factory and trudged through the icy streets of the city. Snow fell around them. It landed softly on their hair as they walked.

"Thanks for saving me, Blink," Nim said.

"I owed you one. I would have died in the cold-storm if you hadn't let me stay in the factory."

The two of them continued to walk through the dark city. Eventually, they reached a road. One way led to Nim's chimney, and the other way led to Blink's.

"Can I tell you something?" Blink asked before they went their separate ways.

Nim didn't usually listen to anything Blink said. But considering he'd just saved her life, she thought it only fair to listen to him tonight.

"I didn't do it."

"Do what?" Nim asked.

"Steal Snot's coat. Well, I didn't steal it how everyone thinks I did."

"Stealing from another tattercoat is never okay," Nim said. "And stealing a coat, of all things, when you already have one of your own, makes it even worse. It's unforgivable."

"Is it still unforgivable if Snot asked me to take it?"

"What do you mean? Why would Snot have asked you to do that?"

"That night was the coldest night we'd ever felt. You know Snot had always been sick: coughing and sneezing and rubbing gunk from his nose. But during the coldstorm he was sicker than usual. Remember?"

Nim thought back to the last time she had seen Snot. It had been two days before he died. He had looked more unwell than normal. His coat had hung off his body, his eyes had been sunken, and green snot had dripped from his nose like water from a tap.

"What does that have to do with you stealing his coat?"

"Snot was already sick that night, and the cold was making him sicker. He said to me that if he died during the night, he wanted me to take his coat. I told him I wouldn't do it; he was my best friend. But then it happened. He stopped sniffling and sneezing and shivering beside me. He just stopped altogether.

"I saw Snot freeze to death, Nim. It was the scariest thing I've ever seen. He just stopped moving and went cold and blue. I keep having this dream. I dream that Hodeldorf keeps getting colder and colder until one day it's so cold that all of us end up like Snot: lying frozen and still in the street."

Nim shivered. She'd often had a similar dream.

"I still didn't want to take his coat," Blink said. "I didn't take it for hours. But I was getting colder and colder, and I didn't want what happened to him to happen to me. I was scared, Nim. I was scared I was going to die. So I took his coat. And it worked. When the sun rose, Snot was still gone, but I was here."

"Why didn't you tell us this before?" Nim asked. If he had told the true story, he might never have been kicked out of the tattercoats.

"I tried," Blink said. "I tried to tell you all the truth. But no one would listen. You just expelled me and said you'd never speak to me again. Besides, I felt like I'd done the wrong thing too, even though it was what Snot had asked. I was his best friend, Nim. I shouldn't have taken anything from him. Not even when he was dead."

Nim felt sorry for Blink, but she was also confused.

"That doesn't explain why you keep stealing coats."

"I was thrown out of the tattercoats, so I don't have to follow the code anymore. When I get cold, I steal another coat to keep warm."

"I wish you hadn't stolen Otto's coat," Nim said.

At the mention of Otto, Blink realized the boy was missing.

"They didn't snatch him too, did they?"

Nim shook her head. "He's gone into the woods to find his mother." In the past, Nim would have left it at that. Who needed to know the whole truth? But she cared about Otto. And she was too worried to stay silent. She had to tell someone the truth. "He asked me to go with him, but I said no. I was too scared. But I'm still scared, even just staying here. I'm scared that Otto isn't going to come back. I'm scared he's going to die like Snot. I'm scared it will be my fault. I've broken the code, Blink. A tattercoat was in need, and I didn't help."

Blink thought about what Nim had just said. "Maybe there's still time. When did he leave?"

"About an hour ago."

Blink smiled. "We're the two fastest tattercoats in the city. If anyone can catch up to him, it's us."

"I'm not so sure," Nim said. She was still scared.

"Come on, Nim. It's what a true tattercoat would do. We'll save him, and then we'll figure out a way to save Skid and Roe."

Nim knew Blink was right. Otto needed their help, and they couldn't do anything to help Skid and Roe right now. She couldn't let Otto down. So instead of going back to her chimney, she followed Blink to the edge of the city.

Chapter Twenty-One

THE OLD TREE STUMP

When Nim and Blink reached the gates of Hodeldorf, they stopped. The forest loomed before them. As Nim stared at the giant trees, a fresh wave of fear washed over her. She knew every street in Hodeldorf. She knew which ones were safe to pass through during the day, which ones you could slip along at night, and which ones you should never enter at all. In the woods, she wouldn't know anything. This was a very bad idea.

Before Nim could turn away, Blink pulled her toward the trees. They left the city behind and stepped into the woods. A deep shadow fell over them. Nibbles left Nim's shoulder and scurried into her pocket.

The forest was dark and quiet. Trees loomed up around them. All sounds of the city faded away. The branches were so thick they blocked the snow from falling. This place didn't feel like any place in Hodeldorf. It felt wild and dangerous. While they couldn't see anyone else, it felt like there were thousands of things all around them, watching silently as these new visitors entered their world.

Nim and Blink walked deeper into the trees. The city fell out of sight. A worn path led them farther into the woods.

"I guess we should follow the path, right?" Nim said. "If we don't take a break, maybe we'll find Otto tonight."

"How do you know he followed the path?" Blink asked. The sun was beginning to set. Purples and oranges trickled through the branches and fell across the forest floor.

"Well, I don't know for sure," Nim admitted. "But it's a good place to start."

Nim soon realized it was going to be a lot trickier than that. A second path appeared, branching off the first, and then a third twisted off between the trees. Soon, they'd passed over twenty different paths and searched down several of them in the hope of finding her missing friend.

"Otto?" Nim called for what felt like the hundredth time. "Otto, where are you?"

"Forget where he is," Blink said. "What about us? I think we're lost."

"We'll just have to keep walking," Nim said. "If we walk for long enough, we're sure to find something."

Two more hours passed. The sun set, and the moon rose. Blink pulled a lantern from his bag to light the way. Nim was very glad he'd stolen that. The light shone on the giant trees around them but cast everything else into shadow. As the lantern swayed in Blink's hand, the trees seemed to move. The shadows moved as well, as though someone or something was following them.

Nim and Blink continued to trek through the woods. No matter which way they walked, the trees all looked the same, and no matter how loudly they called out his name, Otto never replied. Eventually, Nim noticed a change up ahead. In among the large forest trees was an old tree stump.

"What are you doing?" Blink asked when Nim sat down on the stump.

"Taking a break. My legs hurt."

"I have a bad feeling about this," Blink said. "Why's there a tree stump in the middle of the woods?"

"It was probably chopped by one of the woodcutters."

Nim had just remembered that the woodcutters only felled trees on the edge of the woods when the stump trembled and rose into the air—all while Nim was still sitting on it.

"What's happening?" Nim said as the stump continued to grow.

"I think it's magical," Blink said.

"Magical things don't exist," Nim yelled. By now she was so high she could barely see Blink.

The stump stopped growing. Nim hoped it would shrink, but as the minutes ticked by the tree stump didn't move. She was stuck.

Nim peered down and gulped. She had never been afraid of heights. Once, she'd even danced on the Vidlers' roof when they went out for dinner. But she was now ten times higher than the Vidlers' roof. If she slipped, she wouldn't survive the fall. As if Nim weren't scared enough, a crack appeared at the top of the stump. A little green vine began to creep out. It reached across the old wood and wrapped itself around Nim's shoe. It spun itself around Nim's foot three times and then began to pull. To Nim's horror, a small hole appeared in the trunk beneath her feet and began to grow wider. It was like the tree was trying to eat her.

"Help, Blink!" Nim screamed into the night. "Help! It's going to eat me!"

Nim's screams trickled down to the forest floor. Blink couldn't see what was happening but he knew it wasn't good. He searched his bag for something that would help. He couldn't find anything in there, but he did own something else.

For years, Blink had stolen coats. Now he might have another use for them. He took off his coats quickly and laid them on the ground. As each one fell away, cold leached into his bones.

Blink had taken so many coats he couldn't remember most of the steals. But he could recall the thrill of getting his hands on the finest green coat he had ever seen, the shame and sadness and desperation of taking Snot's coat, and the pride he had felt when he'd stolen his first one many years ago and been welcomed into the tattercoats.

Blink wouldn't survive without a coat. So he kept the newest and warmest one—Otto's emerald-green one—and used a small knife to cut the other coats into strips. He started tying the strips together as fast as he could, and when he was finished, he had a rope made of broken coats.

"Don't worry, Nim!" he called up to the girl trapped in the night sky. She had been screaming this whole time. "You'll be down soon."

"Hurry!" Nim yelled.

Blink held one end of the rope and threw the other into the sky. It rose halfway up the stump before falling back down. He threw it up again, but it failed to reach Nim. He realized he couldn't do this on his own. Luckily, someone came to help.

Gripping the bark, Nibbles scurried down the

trunk. He grabbed one end of the rope in his teeth and jumped back onto the stump. Weighed down by the rope of coats, he slowly climbed back up to Nim. Nibbles tied the rope around the top of the stump. He nuzzled into Nim's neck for a moment, as if telling her it would be okay, and dove back into her pocket.

By now the vine had wrapped itself halfway up Nim's leg, and the hole in the trunk was large enough for her to fall through. She used her hands to rip apart the vine. But each time she tore a strand away, another would take its place. Realizing Nim still needed help, Nibbles left her pocket and began to nibble at the vines himself. Together, they were able to cut the plant so quickly the vines didn't have time to grow back.

Nibbles dove back into Nim's pocket, and with shaky hands, Nim grabbed the rope. She lowered herself over the edge and slowly began to climb down. Very carefully at first, but then a little quicker as her confidence grew, Nim edged down the giant tree stump. Less than two minutes after leaving the top, she had reached the bottom.

The moment Nim's feet touched the ground, the tree stump shrank, and within five seconds, it looked as small and innocent as it had when they had first seen it.

"I told you I had a bad feeling about it," Blink said as he untied the rope of coats and stuffed the strips in his bag. "And I told you it was magical."

"It was very odd," Nim admitted. "But that doesn't mean it was magical. It's probably just a rare type of tree."

"A rare type of tree that's *magical*," Blink said, emphasizing the final word.

While Nim refused to agree on that point, she did agree to something else. "It might not have been the smartest thing to do. But it did have one positive. I could see all the way across the woods from up there. There's a clearing nearby. Hopefully, we'll be safe there tonight."

And with that, they set off in the direction Nim had spotted.

Chapter Twenty-Two

THE YELLOW COTTAGE

Darkness lay thick upon the forest by the time Nim and Blink reached the clearing in the woods. The moon shone through the opening in the trees and lit up a bright yellow cottage standing in its center. Nim hadn't seen it from above, but she was very glad to see it now. Friendly puffs of smoke rose from a chimney on the roof.

"We could sleep next to that tonight," Nim said.

A white fence ran around the cottage. They opened the gate and tiptoed over to a window. Blink had just stepped onto the windowsill and was about to climb onto the roof when the door to the cottage opened.

"Who's there?" said an old lady. Her face was twisted like an ancient tree. Her body was too: her back was bent, and her fingers were so swollen they could barely clutch her walking stick. A large coat, at least three sizes too big, kept her warm. Ten bare toes peeked out from beneath the cloth.

"Err . . ." Blink jumped down from the window-sill. "We were just, um . . ." He looked to Nim for help.

"Looking for a place to sleep," Nim said truthfully. "We were going to sleep on your roof, if that's okay. We'll be very quiet, and we'll leave at dawn. You won't even know we're here."

"Of course you can't sleep on my roof," the woman snapped. "I'd never let a child sleep outside at night. It's dangerous. You can sleep in here with me. The fire's nice and warm tonight."

Nim's eyes lit up. She'd never been allowed to sleep beside a fire before. She peered behind the old lady. The cottage looked warm and bright. A fire blazed in one corner, and colorful rugs covered the dirt floor. They would be a lot more comfortable to sleep on than roof tiles. She began walking toward the front door, but Blink pulled her back.

"I've got a bad feeling about this," Blink whispered. "Just like I had with the tree stump. I think we should go."

"Oh boohoo," the old woman said to Blink with a scowl. She must have overheard him. "You're no fun at all!" She turned to Nim and smiled. Most of her teeth were rotten. "What harm is there in staying here for one night? There are two of you and only one of me. You are young and strong. I am old and weak. Come to think of it, I should be the one more scared of you. Best be keeping on your way."

The old woman edged inside. Before she closed the door, Nim noticed what she was wearing.

"Wait. Please," Nim called out. "We won't hurt you. You won't even notice we're here."

"All right, then," the old woman said. "You've convinced me. Come inside. I'm just serving dinner."

"Are you mad?" Blink whispered as Nim walked toward the door. "It might be dangerous."

"Just trust me," Nim whispered back.

When Nim and Blink entered the cottage, they found the table already set for three. It was like the old lady had been waiting for them.

"Please, have a seat and eat with me," the old woman said. She introduced herself as Islebill.

Nim and Blink sat down at the table. Even though the bread was slightly stale and the soup was slightly cold, they were grateful for both. The food tingled in their mouths as they ate. Nim was eating the last bit of her soup when Islebill asked them for a favor.

"Could you two dears help an old lady clear the table?"

Grateful they didn't have to sleep outside, Nim and Blink did as they were asked. But the requests didn't end there. After clearing the table, Nim and Blink had to wash and dry the dishes and then wash the table itself. Just when they thought the chores were done, Islebill asked Nim for another favor.

"Be a dear, little Nim, and sweep the floor. My back's too old and crooked to clean it myself."

While Nim swept the floor, Islebill asked Blink to clean the windows. He scrubbed every window inside the cottage and was about to clean the outside when he realized he couldn't. He pulled at the doorknob, but it wouldn't budge. The front door was locked. Blink's sense of dread grew. He wondered why Nim had been so eager for them to come inside. He hoped it was worth it. And he equally hoped she had a plan to ensure they would be able to leave.

"I always keep it locked at night," Islebill said when Blink continued to pull on the handle. "There are evil, wicked things out there in the woods. Wicked things you must keep out at all costs. You can wash the outside of the windows tomorrow."

By now, Nim had swept the entire floor except for a small patch near Islebill's feet. As she went to brush around them, Nim noticed Islebill's toes were covered in hairy warts. Nibbles, who had poked his head out of Nim's pocket to inspect her work, squealed with fright.

"Yum," Islebill said when she saw Nibbles. She smacked her lips together. "I love rats, particularly their tails." She made a strange slurping sound with her tongue. "Back in the golden years of these woods, you'd see hundreds of them scampering up into the trees. When true winter fell, they started to run into the houses to keep warm. I lived off rat stew for a good twenty years."

Nibbles shuddered and retreated into Nim's pocket.

"Well, you won't be eating Nibbles," Nim said. "He's a special rat: not at all for eating."

"That's a shame," Islebill said. "You wouldn't think it, but rats are awfully tasty. And I'm sure the special ones are even tastier. Now, I think that's enough cleaning for tonight. You can help me with a few more chores tomorrow. I'll be offering breakfast and tea in the morning and a small meal"—she glanced at Nim's pocket—"in the midst of the day."

Nim and Blink spent the night sleeping on the floor in front of the fire. Islebill snored in the room beside them.

"She snores worse than a man," Blink whispered to Nim. "Worse than a man who snores really loudly."

It was true. The snores were so loud they almost drowned out the sound of the wolves howling in the woods.

"I don't think this was a good idea," Blink said. "What if she keeps us locked in here forever?"

"We had no choice," Nim replied.

"Yes, we did. We could have left, walked away before we even came inside."

"No, we couldn't do that."

"Why not?" Blink hissed.

"Because of her coat."

"Huh?" Blink hadn't expected that answer.

"What color is her coat?" Nim said.

Blink searched his memory. "Red?"

"Not just red. Red with a white fur trim. Islebill was wearing Otto's mother's coat. How did she get that? Maybe it's not just Otto who needs our help. Maybe his mother does too."

Chapter Twenty-Three

THE RED COAT

"That's a lovely coat," Nim said to Islebill the following morning over breakfast. Despite their having watched Islebill prepare their porridge fresh, the goop that was served to them tasted over a week old.

"It is," Islebill replied as she shoveled more porridge into her mouth. "Though if the woods weren't so cold I wouldn't need one," she added grumpily.

"Did you make it yourself?" Nim asked as she took a hesitant mouthful of the porridge. It made her mouth tingle even more than the night before.

"It doesn't matter how I got it, only that I have it," Islebill snapped. "And it does a good job of keeping me warm. Now, up you get. You've got more chores to do."

At Islebill's urging, Nim and Blink continued to

clean the cottage. Islebill even made them climb onto the roof and scrub the tiles. When they were finished, they returned inside.

"Islebill?" Nim called. The old lady was nowhere in sight.

"Maybe we should leave," Blink whispered. "Get out of here while she isn't looking."

"We can't just leave," Nim said. "Somehow she's got Otto's mother's coat. She might still be here. Otto as well."

"If Otto's mother was still here, she'd still be wearing her coat," Blink said. "Something bad must have happened. If we stay, it might happen to us too."

"Don't be so dramatic," Nim said.

Nim entered Islebill's bedroom. Blink reluctantly followed. There was no sign of the old lady. Her bed was made, and two cupboards stood in the corner.

"She must have gone into the woods," Nim said. "Come on. Let's search her room."

Nim looked under the bed. There was nothing there. She opened the first cupboard. It was crammed with clothes. She pulled the clothes out and laid them on the bed.

"I don't think those belong to Islebill," Blink said. When Nim had finished putting the items out, eight outfits—coats, pants, and shoes—lay before them. They were men's clothes and looked very old.

As Nim looked at the eight sets of clothes, a

sick idea came to mind. "Do you think these clothes belonged to those woodcutters?" she asked. "The ones who disappeared?"

Blink studied the clothes. They looked just the type to be worn by woodcutters: thick fur-lined coats, chunky boots, and an extra piece of leather sewn into the pants to hold an axe. Judging by their condition, they could very well have been fifty years old.

"What do you think happened to them?" Blink asked.

But before Nim could answer, the second cupboard moved.

Nim and Blink jumped with fright.

"Do you think they're in there?" Nim whispered.

The cupboard door flew open. Islebill stepped down into the room. When she noticed the two children standing next to her, she, too, jumped with fright. Then her eyes narrowed in on the clothes.

"Put those away," she said. "And get back to work."

"We've already finished the roof," Nim replied. "We thought we'd clean your room."

"I don't want you to clean my room. Put those clothes back in the cupboard, or I'll lock the two of you in there instead."

Nim and Blink did as they were told and hid the clothes away. As Nim crammed them in, she glanced at the second cupboard and swore she saw a light inside.

Islebill noticed her line of sight and quickly kicked the other cupboard closed.

"That's better," Islebill said when the clothes had been put away. "Now, out you go and clean the walls. I've got work to do in here."

Nim and Blink went back outside. Instead of cleaning the walls, they peered through the bedroom window. They were just in time to see the old lady climb back into the second cupboard.

"What do you think she's doing?" Blink asked. "You can't do much inside a cupboard."

"It isn't a cupboard," Nim replied. "Before she closed the door, I saw inside. There are steps in there. They must lead down to a cellar. I bet that's where she's keeping Otto's mother. Maybe the woodcutters and Otto are in there too."

That night, when Islebill was snoring loudly in her bed, Nim and Blink sneaked into her room. They crossed the floor and opened the second cupboard.

Nim climbed in first. A thin staircase led down into the earth. Nim used Blink's lantern to light the way. Slowly, a room came into sight.

"Are they in there?" Blink whispered as he climbed down behind her.

"I don't think so," Nim said. "It looks empty."

A table stood in the center of the room. Bundles of dried flowers and herbs covered the surface. Shelves lined every wall. The shelves were full of bottles.

"What do you think is inside?" Blink asked.

Nim approached the nearest shelf and looked at the bottle. It held a purple liquid. The label on the front said OWL.

"What does that mean?" Blink asked when Nim read out the name.

Nim shrugged and moved on to the next bottle.

"'Wolf,'" she said, reading out the label. "And this one here"—she picked up a bottle containing a green liquid—"is called 'Mouse.'"

Most of the bottles were labeled with the names of animals. Some were labeled with other words, like HONESTY and DEATH. Nim was just picking up a small bottle that contained a clear liquid when she realized someone else was in the cellar.

"Hello, dears," Islebill said.

Nim jumped and dropped the bottle. The glass smashed. Liquid spilled onto the dirt. It sizzled, and the ground beneath it turned black.

"What are these things?" Blink asked Islebill, nodding toward the bottles.

"They're my potions. I can magic up ten a day."

"Magic?" Nim said. "Magic isn't real." But even as she said the words, Nim was starting to doubt them.

While there wasn't that much that was magical about Hodeldorf, she was beginning to realize there were quite a few magical things surrounding it.

"Yes, it is," Islebill said. "I'm a witch: the magical witch of the woods."

"Prove it," Nim said.

"I will," Islebill replied. "Once you finish your chores, I'll gobble the both of you up. I think I'll make you a wolf," she said to Blink, "for a hearty wolf stew. And you"—she nodded to Nim—"will be a chicken. You can't beat a bowl of fresh chicken soup."

As she looked at all the potions stacked around her—potions that turned humans into animals—a horrible feeling fell upon Nim.

"Is that what you did to Marta?" she said. Had Otto's mother been eaten months ago?

"Marta?" Islebill frowned. "Who's that?"

"The woman whose coat you stole."

"This old thing?" Islebill held out the skirt of her coat. "I didn't steal this. I traded it."

"What do you mean?"

"Every full moon, the traveling salesman stops at my cottage. I give him some of my potions, and in return he gives a few little things to me."

"So you didn't eat Marta?"

"Eat her?" Islebill said. "I've never even heard of her. Now get out of my cellar and go to bed."

"Forget bed," Nim said when Islebill had shut the door to her room. "We're getting out of here."

Now that they were certain Otto and his mother weren't in the yellow cottage, it was time for them to leave. Islebill was not a kind old lady. She wasn't even a nasty old lady. She was a witch: a witch who wanted to magic them into animals and then gobble them up. She'd probably gobble up Nibbles as well when she was finished eating them. They grabbed their things and headed toward the front door.

"It's locked," Blink said when he tried the handle.

They checked the windows. They were locked too.

"We'll have to break our way out," Nim said. She grabbed the fire iron from the fireplace and slammed it against the window above the sink. Nothing happened.

"Here. Give me a go." Blink took the fire iron and drew it over his shoulder. Then he swung it forward with all his might. Again, the window remained unbroken. It didn't even have a scratch.

"Why isn't it working?" Nim asked.

"Because it's a magic window."

Nim and Blink spun around. Islebill stood in the doorway to her bedroom. She was wearing Marta's coat.

"Well, open it," Nim said. "We want to leave."

"You're not going anywhere," Islebill remarked. "I haven't had wolf stew in over fifty years, and it's been over a decade since I had chicken soup. The cold might be making me weaker, but I'm still strong enough to eat the two of you."

Nim snatched the fire iron from Blink and ran toward Islebill. She raised it above her head. Forget hitting the window; she was going to hit the witch. But as she drew the fire iron down, it flew out of her grasp and into the open hand of Islebill.

"That wasn't very nice of you, dear," Islebill said. "Not very nice at all."

Nim backed away from Islebill. She stopped when she stood beside Blink.

"Please let us go," Nim said.

Islebill cackled. "Not a chance."

She raised the fire iron to her mouth and whispered something to it. Then she threw it in the air.

The fire iron twirled across the room. As it moved, the iron it was made from began to change. It grew thinner and longer until it resembled a long piece of gray string. Then it threaded itself back together in the form of a cage. The cage fell down around Nim and Blink. It hit the ground with a heavy thud. They were trapped. A final piece of the iron broke off and flew back into Islebill's hand. It was a key.

BACAWK!

Nim and Blink pulled on the bars of the cage. Even though the bars were as thin as string, they were strong and heavy. They tried to lift the cage off the ground, but it wouldn't move.

Islebill laughed.

"You won't be getting out of there without this." She held up the iron key before slipping it into her pocket.

Certain the children couldn't escape, Islebill went to fetch some things from her cellar. When she returned, she held two potions. One was labeled WOLF; the other was labeled CHICKEN.

"I'll be having a very fine feast tomorrow," Islebill said as she walked past their cage. She put the potions on the kitchen counter, next to the porridge she had left soaking overnight.

✦ 173 ✦

"I'll have sweet dreams now: sweet dreams of eating the two of you." She smacked her lips together and went back to bed.

"Are you regretting coming to this cottage now?" Blink whispered when the witch was snoring in her bed.

"Of course I am," Nim snapped. "But there's no point whining about that. We have to get out of here."

The cage had trapped not only them, but also their bags. They searched through these now, trying to find something that would help them escape.

Just then, Nibbles pulled on Nim's sleeve. "Not now," Nim whispered to Nibbles as she searched through her things. "We don't have much time. Islebill will be awake in a few hours, and then she'll eat us."

Nibbles kept pulling on Nim's sleeve. Nim was about to tell him off again, when she realized something. While the bars of the cage were too close together for herself or Blink to slip through, they were easy for a rat to get past.

"That's what you were trying to tell me, wasn't it?" Nim said to her furry friend.

Nibbles nodded.

"What are you talking about?" Blink whispered.

"Nibbles can get through the cage. He can save us."

"How's he going to do that? If he tries to steal the key and Islebill catches him, she'll kill him and eat him as well."

Nim knew Blink was right. They would have to figure out a different plan. She looked around the room. When her eyes fell on the potions and the porridge sitting beside them, she had an idea. She didn't even have to say it; Nibbles knew exactly what was on her mind. He gave a sharp nod and set off for the kitchen.

Nibbles scurried along the floor of the cottage and up onto the counter. He pulled the stopper off the first potion and poured it down the sink. Then he rinsed it out in one of the buckets of water Islebill kept beside the fire. He used the other bucket to fill the jar up. He pushed the stopper back in and returned it to the counter.

"Great work, Nibbles," Nim said. "Now do the same to the other one."

Nibbles removed the second stopper. Just before he poured the potion away, Blink had an idea.

"Don't pour it in there," he said. "Pour it into the porridge."

Nibbles twitched his whiskers and looked at Nim. Nim nodded an okay. Nibbles tipped the potion into the bowl of porridge. Then he rinsed the bottle out and filled it with water. He pushed the lid back into place, gave the porridge a quick stir, and scurried back to their cage.

✦ ✦ ✦

"Yum-yum. Eat up," Islebill said to Blink the following morning as she held the bottle labeled WOLF beneath his nose. "Don't be frightened. It's very tasty."

Blink pretended he was scared. He clamped his mouth shut and looked away.

"Don't make me force it down," Islebill said.

Blink slowly opened his mouth, and the witch poured the liquid.

Islebill placed the empty bottle on the counter. She picked up the second one and held it out to Nim.

"You too, dear. Drink away."

Nim didn't wait as long as Blink. She gulped the liquid in one go.

"How long does it take?" she asked Islebill as she handed her the empty bottle through the cage.

"A few minutes. Once you're ready, I'll chop you both up and put you on to boil. I'll have the chicken for lunch and the wolf for dinner. I'll have enough left-overs for weeks."

While she waited for her lunch and dinner to morph into shape, Islebill scooped her porridge into a bowl. She sat down at the kitchen table alone and began to eat.

By the time Islebill had finished her first bowl of porridge, nothing had happened.

"That's strange," she said. She served herself another bowl. She was halfway through that one when she grew concerned. "Something's wrong," she said. "You should be changing by no—bacawk!"

Islebill clamped her hand over her mouth. She looked down at her bowl of porridge and clucked again.

"No. No. No," Islebill said. She jumped up from the table and ran over to the counter. She smelled her porridge and frowned. Then she smelled the two empty bottles. They held no scent of potion. She turned to Nim and Blink. "You switched the—bacawk! Bacawk! Bacawk!"

Islebill clucked about the kitchen for a few seconds. Then several feathers sprouted out of her head. She suddenly grew very short, and her legs became covered in scales.

"I need the remedy," she said. "I need the reversing potion." She began to run toward her bedroom. As she did, her arms shrank away and wings took their place.

"Bacawk! Bacawk!" she screamed as she ran around in circles. Her coat pooled on the ground around her, pulling at her legs.

"Quick, Nibbles," Nim yelled. "Now's your chance."

Nibbles ran out of the cage and over to the coat. He darted about the angry chicken, checking every pocket of the coat until he found the iron key. He raced back to the cage and put it in the lock. The key turned, and the cage clicked open. Nim and Blink grabbed their bags and climbed away from the bars.

By now, Islebill was almost entirely a chicken. The only human-looking part left was her nose. It appeared her brain was still working too. Realizing her prey was about to escape, she bolted toward her second cupboard and jumped inside. She was going to get the reversing potion.

"Now's our chance," Blink said.

They ran toward the door. Islebill had unlocked it that morning. They raced out into the frosty morning air and bolted down the garden path. Nim kicked the gate open, and they raced off into the woods.

A few minutes later, they heard a woman call faintly through the trees: "Come back here, dears!" But they were so far from the cottage the witch didn't have the power to magic them back.

Chapter Twenty-Five

THE WOODLAND WOLVES

A new day dawned as Nim and Blink left the witch's cottage behind. Weak sunlight filtered through the trees. For the rest of the day, Nim and Blink searched the woods for their missing friend. Free from the scary gaze of Islebill, Nibbles sat on Nim's shoulder. His delicate whiskers twitched back and forth as he sought out the scents of the forest.

"Can you smell Otto?" Nim asked.

Nibbles shook his head. He couldn't sniff out a single boy in the vast woods.

"Never mind," Nim said. "We'll have to find him another way."

By the time night fell, they had found no trace of Otto. He had disappeared just like his mother.

"Well, at least we're a long way from Islebill's cottage," Nim said, trying to find a positive.

"I guess," Blink replied. He was staying close to Nim. The woods were scary at night. The wind moaned through the branches and swirled around their ears; the trees moved like giant ghosts; and, once in a while, the lone cry of an owl would pierce the air and make them jump.

With no warm chimney to sleep beside, they snuggled up against a tree. It creaked and groaned in the cold wind, as if trying to speak to them: perhaps warning them to get away. They used Blink's torn coats for a blanket.

Nim and Blink took turns keeping watch. But by the middle of the night, exhausted from a day of walking, they were both fast asleep. Even Nibbles couldn't keep his eyes open.

Several hours passed. Occasionally, an owl would hoot nearby and wolves would howl faintly through the trees. Then, the howls grew very close and the hooting stopped.

"What's that?" Blink said. The howls had pulled him awake.

"I don't know," Nim whispered, rubbing sleep from her eyes. "You were keeping watch."

"No, I wasn't. It was your turn."

Nim was still arguing with Blink when Nibbles

pulled on her coat. The rat pointed over her shoulder. Nim turned around.

Seven wolves stood before them. They bared their teeth and growled.

"Oh no," Blink said. "They're going to eat us. This is worse than being at Islebill's."

The wolves growled louder and moved closer.

"Islebill?" The word came from the mouth of the middle wolf. He was speckled gray and tan, and larger than the others.

"It can talk," Blink squeaked.

"We all can," said another wolf.

"Are you friends of Islebill?" the speckled one asked. He was the leader.

"Friends?" Anger took away some of Nim's fear. "Of course not. She trapped us in her cottage. We only just escaped."

The wolf studied Nim's face and sniffed the air. It was like the wolf was trying to sniff out a lie. Not finding one, his hackles dropped.

"We are not friends of Islebill's either," the leader said. "Fifty years ago, she trapped us in her cottage. Back then, we were men: woodcutters from Hodeldorf. She welcomed us into her cottage when we got lost and offered us a warm meal. She wanted to make wolf stew, but she didn't have any wolf meat. So she magicked us into wolves and used my own axe to chop poor Wilhelm up."

The other wolves howled at the moon in sadness at the loss of their friend.

"We escaped before she could eat us," said a wolf as white as the moon. "We had hoped her magic would fade when we got away. But it hasn't. We're just getting older and slower and colder. We're dying as wolves, but we were born as men."

"I'm so sorry," Nim said.

"We thought Islebill might be behind all of this," said the lead wolf.

"Behind what?" Nim asked.

"Behind the winter that doesn't end."

"The cold that doesn't lift," said the white wolf.

"The failing sun," said a black wolf standing to the left. "The days are getting shorter, and the nights are getting longer. Soon, it will be dark forever."

"The woods are losing their magic too," the lead wolf said. "Years ago, when our fathers' fathers walked these woods, they were warm, and blossoms covered the ground instead of snow. Back then, even the trees in the forest were magical. But the woods have been dying for many, many years. And the magic is dying with them."

"Why would Islebill make it cold when the cold makes her weak?" Nim said. "It has to be something else."

"None of the creatures here know what it is," said the white wolf. "But they all agree on one thing.

A woodland creature isn't behind this. Humans are making the world dark."

"How can you be sure?" Nim said.

"Because people are behind all the bad things that happen in the woods. The felling of the trees: we, ourselves, did that. The burning of the bark. The killing of our wolfkind to make those things you wear to keep warm." The wolf nodded toward Nim's and Blink's coats. He had been away from humans for so long he had forgotten what they were called. "It's so cold even our own fur doesn't keep us warm."

Nim knew there were a lot of nasty people in Hodeldorf, like the storekeepers who beat tattercoats out of their stores, like thieves who robbed anyone of everything, and like homeowners who kicked children off their roofs when they had nowhere else to go. But there was only one person she could think of who would be cruel enough to do this.

"I bet it's Frau Ferber," she said.

"Frau Ferber?" asked the lead wolf. "Who's that?"

"A nasty old lady who locks poor children in her factory and uses them to make herself rich: rich off the sale of boot polish. But it can't be her. Why would she want to make Hodeldorf cold? She doesn't like the cold more than anyone else. There's something we're missing . . ."

"We are missing it too," said the lead wolf.

"Perhaps if we found what we were missing—what we have lost—the world would grow warm once more." He looked sadly at the ground. When he raised his eyes, there was a flicker of hunger in them. He stepped closer before shaking his head and edging away.

"We should be off," said the wolf. "The longer we stay as wolves, the less we are like men. One day soon, I fear we will start hunting humans to eat."

"Wait," Blink called as they turned to walk away. "Wait just a bit longer. I have something to give you."

Blink untied the strips of cloth that had made their blanket. Using a needle and thread from her bag, Nim helped to stitch them back together. It was a tricky job, and they didn't have enough time to do it neatly. Some pieces got mixed up, and some edges didn't match. When they were finished, they had seven patchy coats for seven patchy wolves.

"These will keep you warm," Blink said.

"And remind you that you are still men," Nim added, "even if sometimes you forget."

"Thank you," said the lead wolf as he admired his new coat. "You are kind for humans."

The wolves were about to leave for a second time when Nim realized they might be able to help with something else.

"Have you seen any others of our kind lately?" she asked. "A boy and a lady perhaps?"

The seven wolves shook their heads.

"We've wandered very far," said their leader. "We haven't been in this part of the woods for years. If we do see them, would you like us to eat them?"

"Oh no!" Nim said. "Don't do that. If you see them, could you tell them their friends are looking for them?"

"We can keep a nose out for them," the lead wolf said. "But we don't know what they smell like."

"Like this." Blink took off Otto's coat and held it out to the wolves.

The wolves sniffed the cloth. They could smell the scent of Blink, the scent of the boy who had worn it before, and the faint scent of the woman who had stitched it.

"We will look out for them," the lead wolf promised. Then the pack was off, bounding through the tall woods in their new tatty coats.

"Well, they were rather nice," Blink said.

"I wish we could have given them more than just coats," Nim said. "What do you think, Nibbles?"

Nim looked down at her pocket, but Nibbles didn't look out.

"Nibbles?" Nim said a bit louder. She checked all her pockets. But each one was empty. Nibbles was gone.

Chapter Twenty-Six

THE MAGICAL PIPE

"**D**o you think the wolves took him?" Nim asked as she searched her pockets again.

"I don't think they would have done that," Blink said. He checked his pockets as well. But there was no sign of Nibbles.

"Maybe they did it by accident," Nim said. "Maybe he got stuck in one of their new coats. Wolves!" Nim called. "Wolves, come back. Please! You've taken Nibbles!"

Nim's voice echoed through the woods. But no voices or howls echoed back.

"Maybe he ran away," Blink said.

Nim glared at him. "Nibbles would never do that. I'm his best friend. We haven't left each other's side since we met. Someone must have taken him."

Nim and Blink searched the forest around them. The darkness made it difficult to see, but they continued throughout the night. By morning, in the first light of the rising sun, they could still find no trace of Nibbles.

It wasn't until they stopped thumping about among the trees that they heard a faint sound.

A pipe echoed through the woods. It played a simple, jolly tune.

"It's a rather nice song, isn't it?" Blink said. He was smiling.

"We don't have time for listening to music. We've got more important things to do. We need to find Nibbles, and then we've got to find Otto."

But as Nim leaned down to search for her rat, the tune changed. It grew quicker and louder. Nim forgot all about Nibbles, and she began talking about the song.

"I've never heard one like it. I wonder who's playing it."

"Maybe it's playing itself," Blink said. He began to follow the music.

"What are you doing?" Nim said. She pulled Blink back. "You can't just follow anything you hear. What if it's a trap?"

Blink looked worried for a moment, but then the music grew even louder. A blank smile spread across his face. He pulled free of Nim and walked away. Nim ran after him. She had intended to pull him back, but then the music got ahold of her too. She followed Blink deeper into the woods.

Nim and Blink didn't have a care in the world as they followed the music. After they had walked a long while, a thin, frozen stream appeared up ahead.

The music drifted across the silent river. Nim and Blink followed the stream. With each step they took, the music grew louder, and they forgot about everything else. They forgot about losing Nibbles. They forgot about the seven wolves who used to be men. They forgot about the wicked Islebill and the boy and his mother, whom they had come into the woods to find. They even forgot about Hodeldorf and the tattercoats. It was like the music had slipped into their minds and robbed all other thoughts away.

Eventually, they reached a clearing in the woods. They left the safety of the trees. Even if Islebill's cottage had stood in the center, they would have continued.

With no trees to catch it, snow swirled down into the clearing. A giant shoe, almost as large as a house, filled the space. A little man stood at the top of the shoe, playing a pipe. On the ground nearby sat a rat wearing a sky-blue coat.

Nibbles. He'd heard the music too.

Chapter Twenty-Seven

ODE THE GIANT

E ven though they had originally set off to find Nibbles, Nim and Blink hardly seemed to notice him as they walked closer to the man in the shoe. They were almost beside the rat when Nim trod on a fallen branch. It snapped in two.

As if the spell cast by the music had been broken, the man stopped playing the pipe. He looked at Nim and Blink. Every piece of the man's face looked bigger than it should have been, or slightly the wrong size, like it couldn't decide if it should be big or small. The man had large ears, a small nose, and very large green eyes. His hair was a crown of brown leaves that rustled in the wind.

He smiled when he saw them.

"Hello," he said. Even though he no longer played the pipe, his voice sounded musical.

Now that the pipe had stopped playing, its magic stopped too. In an instant, Nim's thoughts came back to her. The first thought was one of fear. They were in trouble. What did this man want from them? Her second thought was of Nibbles. She had to get him back.

"You took my Nibbles," Nim said.

"Did I?" The man followed Nim's gaze. He seemed to see Nibbles for the first time. "Hello down there," he said. "Aren't you a strange little thing?"

Now that Nibbles was free from the magical pipe, he scurried back to Nim. The man in the shoe did not try to stop him. Nibbles dove into his favorite pocket and let out a little squeak.

"It's not your fault, Nibbles," Nim reassured him. "You didn't mean to come here. That nasty man made you."

"*Man?*" yelled the stranger in the shoe.

Nim and Blink jumped with fright.

"How dare you call me a man? I'm not a man. I'm Ode the Giant."

"You don't look like a giant to me," Blink said. Instantly, he regretted saying that. He didn't want to make this creature—man or giant—angry. Who knew what he was capable of? But he needn't have worried. Ode didn't look angry. He looked sad.

"That is most likely true," Ode said softly. "I

haven't looked like a giant in fifty years. I used to be the largest giant in these woods, perhaps in the entire world. This used to be my shoe, did you know?" He looked down at the gigantic shoe he sat in. "When I walked these woods, every footfall became a clearing, every sneeze fell like rain, and when I went to the toilet, whole rivers were made."

Nim and Blink wished they hadn't heard that last bit.

"Still," Ode said, "it could be worse. I haven't seen my brother and sister in over twenty years. Last time I saw them, Opus was even smaller than your rat, and Odette was the size of a bird. By now they have probably shrunk down to nothing."

Ode raised the pipe to his mouth and began to play a mournful tune. The music swirled among the trees, joining the swirling snow, and the shrinking giant cried. Nim, Blink, and Nibbles cried too. But as soon as the music stopped, so did their tears.

"Luckily, my pipe shrank with me," Ode said. "If I didn't have my pipe to play, I would be awfully lonely."

"Do you play it all the time?" Blink asked.

Ode nodded. "Except when I'm sleeping. Giants need a lot of sleep; that's why we live so long. The oldest giant lived to be eight hundred and ninety-six. I wonder how long I'll live now that I'm small like you."

"About that," Nim said. "Why are you shrinking?"

"It's been happening since winter came and didn't

go away. Before it got cold, I used to stand higher than the highest tree. I only ever came out at night in case the men in the town saw. Once, a giant got too close, and the people stabbed him until he couldn't move. We giants have stayed away from you humans ever since." Ode looked between the two of them and said, "Are you going to hurt me?"

Nim and Blink shook their heads.

"That's a relief." Ode yawned and put his pipe into his pocket.

"How many giants are there?" Nim asked.

"In these woods, there's only me. In about one decade or maybe two, I will be too small to see. I'm not sure what will happen then. Maybe I'll disappear."

By now, Ode was yawning at the end of every sentence.

"It's almost time for me to go to sleep," he explained as his head nodded up and down. "I haven't had this much company in over fifty years. First there was that lonely boy, and then the three of you."

"Lonely boy?" Nim said. She stepped closer to the shrinking giant. "What lonely boy?"

"Just a human one," Ode said sleepily. His eyes were starting to droop, and he began to lie down in his shoe.

"Wait! What did he look like?

"I already told you," Ode said. "He looked human. Like one of you in your tatty coats. He heard my pipe and came to me. When I stopped playing, he asked if I had seen his mother."

"That's Otto!" Nim cried. "When did you see him?"

"Not too long ago. Maybe three setting suns or four."

"Do you know where he went?" Blink said.

"Of course." Ode yawned a very loud yawn. "I took him there."

"Took him where?"

By now, Ode's eyes were closed. In a moment, he would fall asleep. Who knew how long it would take for him to wake back up?

Nim grabbed hold of Ode's shoulders and gave them a shake. The giant opened his eyes.

"Has it been a day of sleep already?" he asked.

"There's no time for sleep," Nim said. She hauled Ode out of his shoe. "Now, come on. You've got to help us find our friend."

Chapter Twenty-Eight:

THE SUMMER WOOD

Armed with a new lead, and with a shrunken giant to guide them, Nim and Blink walked quickly through the woods. Ode led them along the bank of the frozen river as it wove through the trees.

As they walked, Ode told Nim and Blink more about giants.

"People think we're scary because we're big. We don't mean to squash things. It's very hard to walk delicately when you weigh more than ten trees. We're one of the nicest creatures in the woods, like deer and sparrows. Our favorite thing to do is help others."

"Is that why you helped Otto?" Nim asked.

Ode nodded.

"As soon as I stopped playing my pipe one morning, he was there and asked me if I had seen his mother."

Ode paused for a moment to yawn. "I told him I hadn't, but that if she'd become lost anywhere in these woods it would have been in the summer wood."

"The summer wood?" Nim said. "What's that?"

"You'll see for yourself soon enough."

Ode continued to lead them along the river. Whenever he looked like he was about to nod off, Nim broke off a piece of ice from the stream and dropped it down his back.

They walked for several hours. At first, all the woods looked the same. But then things began to change. The river started to thaw and then run. The falling snow stopped, and green leaves sprouted from the trees. They rustled softly in a gentle breeze.

"It's like the woods are coming back to life," Nim said.

"This is how the woods used to be." Ode smiled warmly, like the season had changed not just the woods but also the giant's heart. It also appeared to have woken him up a little bit, and his eyes were no longer drooping. "Slowly, the coldness and darkness moved in. This is the only place it hasn't reached, but some say it's just as bad."

"What do you mean?" Nim asked.

"The summer wood is a dangerous place," Ode said. "It traps you—tricks you into seeing what you most want to see. It makes you think your dreams are real so you don't want to leave. The longer you stay here, the harder it is to go back. If you stay for too long, the lure of the summer wood grows even stronger than my pipe."

Nim and Blink shivered. They didn't like the sound of this. If Otto truly was trapped somewhere in the summer wood, they might become trapped if they tried to find him. Then all three of them would be lost.

But it was the only hope they had of finding their friend, so they let Ode lead them deeper into the summer wood. The air grew warmer as they walked.

"We almost don't need our coats," Nim said to Blink. But they kept them on all the same.

Eventually, they reached another clearing.

"This is where I left your friend," Ode said. "I told him not to go in any farther, but he wouldn't listen."

Bright green grass covered the ground. Little herbs and large flowers bloomed everywhere. The flowers were brighter than all the coats Nim had ever seen. The smells seemed bright as well. She had never smelled scents so fresh and fragrant. These were the scents and sights of summer.

"It's beautiful," Nim said. For the first time in her life, she realized how dull and cold Hodeldorf really was. Instantly, she wanted it to be this warm and bright forever. She did not want to leave.

While Nim had been looking at the colorful

flowers, Blink had been looking for something else.

"Otto isn't here."

"He might be a little farther in," Nim suggested.

"Go in, if you must," Ode said. "But be careful. The deeper you go, the stronger the pull of the woods becomes. I'll wait here. I know exactly what I would find in there, and I won't be able to leave: my brother and sister, standing happy and tall as the trees. I'll wait here and call you back before nightfall. Just listen out for my pipe."

And with that, Nim and Blink crossed over into the summer wood.

Like they had passed through an invisible wall, Nim and Blink left winter behind and stepped, for the first time, into true summer. The air was instantly hot and warm. The grass grew thick and green.

"I didn't know the sun could be this bright," Nim said, nodding toward the sky.

The woods were so hot Nim and Blink began to take off their coats—until a sound from somewhere up ahead made them stop.

"Did you hear that?" Nim said. She stopped walking and held on to Blink's arm.

"Hear what?" Blink listened to the sound of the woods: the rustling of leaves, the buzzing of bees, and the singing of birds. He wasn't sure which sound Nim was referring to.

"Otto," she said.

They both paused and listened. The faint sound of talking drifted through the trees.

"I think that's a very good color," Otto said. "You'll get a good price for that. We'll be able to move into our own house soon."

"He must be talking to his mother," Nim said. "He's found her. Come on. We'll get them both, and then we can go home."

Nim and Blink hurried through the trees. Otto's voice grew louder. His shape appeared up ahead. He sat beside a tree. His bag lay discarded beside him.

"What do you think of this cloth, Mother?" Nim and Blink watched as Otto offered a flower to the empty air.

"Otto?" Nim said. "Who are you talking to?"

Otto laughed. He kept looking at the empty space near the tree.

"Yes, I think so too," Otto said.

"I don't think he can hear us," Blink whispered. "Or see us either." He waved his hand in front of Otto's face. The boy didn't respond.

"How long do you think he's been sitting here?" Nim asked. Otto looked very pale and thin, like he hadn't eaten in days. His hair was dirty, and his clothes were too. But he was happy, happier than Nim had ever seen him.

"Otto?" Nim crouched in front of her friend and said his name again. But the boy didn't reply. She reached out and pulled on his arm. Otto looked around and frowned.

"Nim?" Otto said. He smiled at Nim and frowned at the boy beside her. "Blink? What are you doing here?"

"We've come to rescue you," Blink said.

Otto laughed. "I don't need rescuing. I've found my mother." He pointed to the empty air in front of him. "She got lost in here too. We've been making coats for days. Soon, we'll be able to buy a house and live together again. And it's so warm here we won't even need a fire. You two could live with us as well, couldn't they, Mother?"

"How about we go back to Hodeldorf and live together there?" Blink said. He turned to Nim for support. But the girl was gone.

Nim knew the two people gathering herbs in the woods were her parents the moment she saw them. Even though she had only been little when they died, she still had the memory of her mother's warm brown eyes and her father's smile, which made his whole face light up.

"Mother? Father?" Nim called as she ran toward them.

The man and woman turned around. Their eyes fell upon Nim, and their faces broke into two smiles as bright as the summer sun.

"Elke?" the woman called. "Oh, Elke. Is that really you?"

Nim's mother dropped the herbs she held and ran to her daughter. She scooped Nim into her arms and twirled her in the air.

Nim felt a rush of warmth. A moment later, a second pair of arms hugged her even tighter.

"Oh, Elke." Her father smelled of pine and smoke. "We've been waiting for you for so long. We knew if we just stayed put, you would come and find us."

They let go of Nim and crouched in front of her.

"My, haven't you grown into a fine young lady," Nim's mother said.

"You're almost as tall as me," her father joked.

Nim laughed, but then her face fell.

"Why did you leave me?" she said.

"I'm sorry we got sick," her father replied. "But we're all better now. Elke, we're so sorry we didn't get you from the factory. We tried every door and window for years, but they were locked."

"But we knew you'd be smart enough to escape," her mother said. "We've been getting ready for you to come home. Come and see what we've built."

Nim's parents took her by the hands and led her

through the trees. A cottage appeared up ahead. It had a bright green door and two cheerful round windows, which shone like eyes in the weakening light. A fire burned brightly inside.

"Come now, Elke." Her mother pulled on her hand. "Come inside, and I'll show you your room."

Nim's room was just how she had always dreamed. It was bright and cozy, with a proper bed and a fireplace just to herself. A shelf of books rested along one wall. Nim had a feeling she would be very happy here.

"Mmm," Nim's mother said. "Can you smell that, Elke? I think your father's making sausages."

Nim turned from the fire and looked toward the other room. She sniffed the air, and her stomach rumbled. She was very hungry. As she went to walk into the kitchen, she heard something.

"Can you hear that, Mother?"

"Hear what, dear?"

"The music," Nim said. A bright, cheerful tune filtered through the window.

Nim peered outside. Dusk had fallen over the woods. Birds flew home for the night, and the trees grew still. She thought she saw a man standing between the trees: a man with a pipe and a very oddly shaped face. But when she blinked, he was gone.

"I can't hear anything." Nim's mother closed the curtains. "You must be imagining it."

At the word *imagine*, the music grew louder.

Nim didn't want to listen to the music, but it called to her all the same. She looked at her mother and the bright, warm bedroom they stood in as it all began to fade. The smell of sausages disappeared, and the crackling fire went out. The walls of the cottage melted into nothing. Last to go were Nim's mother and father, like her mind was desperate to latch on to them the most. Within seconds, Nim and Nibbles were alone in the woods.

"Come on, Nim!" a familiar voice called.

Nim turned and looked through the trees. Otto and Blink ran toward her.

"Hurry up," Blink yelled. "It's getting dark."

Reluctantly, Nim joined her friends. The sound of Ode's pipe grew louder as they ran through the trees. The shrunken giant appeared up ahead. The winter woods loomed behind him.

They left the warmth of the summer wood and stepped into a wintry dusk. Snow drifted down all around them. They were back in the real world. They had found their lost friend, but they had yet to find his mother. And after her encounter in the woods, Nim remembered just how painful it was to lose one of those.

Chapter Twenty-Nine

THE TRAVELING SALESMAN

Even though Nim wanted to escape from the woods as quickly as possible, she knew they couldn't leave without helping Otto find his real mother. Thanks to Islebill, she knew just the person who might be able to help.

"Do you know someone called 'the traveling salesman'?" Nim asked Ode when they'd left the summer wood behind. If Islebill had gotten Otto's mother's coat from him, surely he must know something about her disappearance.

"Oh, the traveling salesman isn't a person," Ode said. "He's a nasty old creature who walks the woods, snatching whatever he wants and selling it for a profit. If it's too big to fit inside his bag, he shrinks it down. If he could throw one of his orbs far enough, I bet he'd shrink down the sun itself."

"His orbs?" Nim said.

"That's what he uses to trap things," Ode explained. "He throws one of his magical orbs and whatever it hits shrinks down inside."

"How do we find him?" Otto asked.

"He only appears at night when the moon is full. He follows a well-worn track that shines silver under the stars."

"When's the next full moon?" Blink said.

"In two days."

"What are we going to do till then?" Nim asked.

"Why, you can stay with me."

Despite the lingering smell of dirty feet, it was quite comfortable inside Ode's old shoe. It was also spacious: the size of a house back in Hodeldorf. While they waited for the traveling salesman, they spoke about their time in the woods. Nim and Blink quickly learned Otto's experience had been very different from their own.

"Did you meet any witches?" Nim asked.

"No," Otto said.

"What about wolves?" Blink said. "Did you bump into any of them?"

Otto shook his head.

"Did you sit on any tree stumps?" Nim asked worriedly.

Otto frowned. "What would have happened if I had?"

It turned out, Otto hadn't seen anything they had.

"I did get startled by a deer once. Well, a baby deer. I don't think it was magical. It just skipped away. It was wandering near the stream. Then I found Ode and went to the summer wood. It was wonderful there. I thought I'd done it. I thought I'd finally found my mother. I didn't know a person could feel that happy. Every sad thought and worry was gone. But then I realized none of it was real."

"I'm sorry you didn't really find your mother," Nim said, sharing in Otto's sadness. "I thought I'd found my parents too. At least you still have a chance to find your real mother. Mine's gone forever." A cloud of sadness fell over Nim's face. "What about you, Blink?" Nim said. She'd never asked the other boy about his own parents, and he'd never offered up the information.

"My mother never wanted me, so she gave me to her sister. But after a few years, she didn't want me either. The tattercoats were the only ones who would take me in. Then, when I got kicked out, I didn't have anyone."

"Well, you've got us now," Ode said. "And you're very welcome to visit my shoe anytime."

It seemed almost a shame when the full moon rose and it came time to leave.

"That's the track over there," Ode said.

A thin silver trail had appeared between the trees. It shone as if a piece of the moon itself had fallen to earth.

"What do we do now?" Nim asked.

"We wait."

And wait the four of them did. The moon rose through the trees. The path stretching past them grew brighter. Wolves howled, and owls flew. Finally, the moon passed directly overhead, and a whistling came through the trees.

A man appeared on the path. He carried a little leather bag that bulged at the seams and jiggled as he walked.

As the traveling salesman grew closer, his whistling turned into words.

> *I am the traveling salesman,*
> *The only one in these woods.*
> *And in my little bag,*
> *You'll find all sorts of things.*
> *Like this and that,*
> *And odds and ends,*
> *And beginnings and middles,*
> *And everything in between.*

The salesman passed through the last row of trees

and into their clearing. Nim, Blink, and Otto moved closer to one another. While the man in front of them looked harmless, they had a feeling he wasn't harmless at all.

When the salesman saw the man and three children standing beside the giant shoe, his eyes lit up.

"Customers!" The man clapped his hands. He had long black hair, worn shoes, and a brand-new coat. "What can I get for you all?"

"Do you sell potions?" Nim asked.

"Oh yes," the salesman replied. "Wolf potions. Owl potions. Bee potions." He stepped closer to his new customers and sniffed the air. He nodded to Nim, Blink, and Otto. "You lot are human, yes? But not you." He turned to Ode and watched him closely.

"What about coats?" Otto said. "Do you sell those?"

"It just so happens I do. And I can tell you're in need of new ones." He eyed their tatty coats with distaste. "You must order them one moon in advance, and you can choose the color."

"Do you make them yourself?" Otto asked.

"Of course not. I don't have time to make coats. But I own someone who does. Would you like to buy some?"

"We can't," Nim said. "We don't have any money."

The man's face fell. "What's the point of all of you

if you aren't going to buy anything?" The excitement in his eyes faded, but then returned when he looked at Ode. "I know what you are," he said. "I haven't seen one of your kind for decades. You're a giant. I'd fetch a fine price for you, even already shrunken."

"Well, you're not getting me," Ode said. His voice trembled slightly. For years he'd hidden deep inside his shoe on every full moon so he wasn't seen by the salesman. He should have remained hidden tonight as well. So focused on helping the little humans, he'd forgotten to think of himself.

"Is that so?" The salesman laughed. He reached into his pocket and pulled out a little glass orb. It was the size of an apple and fit easily into his hand.

"No! Don't!" Ode cried.

Nim grabbed Ode and pulled him toward her, trying to get him away from the orb. But it didn't work. The orb hit Ode on the leg. He let out a loud scream, which quickly faded as the giant was sucked inside. Nim had to let go so she wasn't sucked in as well. As she pulled her hand away, something came with it: a magical pipe.

The orb clattered to the ground. Tiny Ode stood trapped in the glass. Blink went to snatch it, but the salesman whistled, and the orb flew back to its owner. He threw it into his bag and clasped it shut.

"Oh, don't look so worried," he said to Nim, Otto,

and Blink. "I'm not going to shrink down any of you. Most humans aren't worth anything. Now, are you sure you won't be buying anything? I own an awful lot."

"Of course we're not going to buy anything!" Nim said. "You just shrank our friend!"

"In that case," the salesman said, "I'd best be going." He waved goodbye and continued along his path.

"We can't let him get away," Otto said as the salesman faded from sight. "I bet he's trapped my mother in one of his orbs. That's why she never came back for me. She's trapped, and we need to get her out."

Otto started to run after the salesman. Nim raced after him and pulled him back.

"Don't worry, Otto," she said. "We don't have to chase him. He's going to come to us."

Nim raised Ode's pipe to her mouth and began to play. Even though she had never played the instrument before, music came out and filtered through the woods.

As Nim played, a rabbit bounced into the clearing. Then a deer bounded into the space, followed by several winter birds. Eventually, the traveling salesman reappeared upon his path.

"How did I get back here?" the salesman said when the music stopped. He stood right in front of Nim.

He looked at the three humans and then down at the pipe.

"Hey," he said. "That's a magical pipe, isn't it? When you play that pipe, it makes things come to you. Give it here."

Nim put the pipe behind her back. "I'm not going to give it to you, but I'd be willing to make a trade."

"For what?" the salesman asked.

"For Ode and Marta."

"Who are they?"

"The shrunken giant," Nim said angrily.

"And my mother!" Otto said. "The best coat maker in all of Dortzig. We know you have her somewhere."

The salesman laughed. "All right. All right. You can have them both, in exchange for that pipe." He held out his hand.

"I don't trust you," Nim said.

"And rightly so," the salesman agreed. "The last time I struck a deal like that, I was left without a sundragon."

"A sundragon?" Nim said. She thought about the story Sage had told them while they were hiding under Frau Ferber's factory. At the time, she had thought it was just that: a story. But Ode had shown her that giants were real, and Islebill had proved that witches were too. Maybe sundragons did exist. And maybe if they could find one, the world might grow warm again. "Could we trade the pipe for one of them as well?"

"You could if I had one," the salesman said. He

was starting to lose his patience. "They're very rare. They've been hunted for centuries. I don't even know if there are any left. Now, are you going to give me the pipe, or will I have to take it?" He reached into his pocket and pulled out one of his orbs. He was about to throw it at Nim when a growl came from the trees.

Ode's pipe hadn't just lured rabbits and deer to the clearing. It had also fallen upon the ears of seven wolves. They'd come close enough to overhear what was happening, and waited for just the right moment to leave the sanctuary of the trees and encircle the salesman.

"Hello, Nim," the lead wolf said. "Who's this?"

"The traveling salesman."

The wolf sniffed the air. "He smells like Islebill. Are you a friend of Islebill's?"

"I wouldn't say a friend," the salesman said. "More like a customer."

"A customer of Islebill's might make for a tasty meal," said another of the wolves.

Instead of looking scared, the traveling salesman looked excited.

"I've never met a pack of talking wolves before. I could fetch a good price for you."

The salesman raised the orb to his shoulder. But before he could throw it, the white wolf pounced and knocked him to the ground. Several orbs fell out of his pocket and rolled across the snow, where they came to rest near Nim's feet. The salesman desperately tried to grab one, but the wolves swatted the orbs away. The pack snarled and moved closer.

With the salesman pinned to the ground, Blink snatched his bag and opened it.

"What are you doing?" the salesman said as Blink searched through the contents. "Put them back," he yelled as the boy began to pull out his orbs. He also found a few of Islebill's potions. "You haven't paid."

Blink pulled out one of the orbs and held it up toward the moonlight. Inside stood a lone tree. He put the orb back and pulled out another. Eventually, he found the orb he sought.

"Ode!" Blink said when he saw the creature that stood inside. He looked down at the little giant, who was now even littler. "How do we get him out?"

The traveling salesman smirked. "Why would I tell you that?"

Nim knew they couldn't risk doing something wrong. If they broke the orb, they might break the giant trapped inside. She needed to discover the truth of how to release him, and luckily she knew just the thing.

Nim searched through the salesman's bag. She wasn't looking for something in an orb, but something he had just traded for. She searched among Islebill's potions until she found the one she sought.

Nim opened the stopper on a jar of purple liquid. The label on the jar read: HONESTY.

"No!" the salesman said when his own eyes read the label. "I won't drink it."

"Yes, you will," Nim said.

While the wolves stood guard, Nim poured the potion into the salesman's mouth. When he had swallowed the purple liquid, Nim began to ask him some questions.

"How do I get Ode out?"

The salesman tried to keep his mouth closed. The longer he kept his mouth closed, the wider his eyes became. Soon, he could hold it in no longer. The truth had to come out.

"Crack it open like an egg," he said. "Three hits on the ground, and then it breaks in two."

Blink did as the salesman said. He knelt and hit the orb on the ground three times. A crack appeared around its center. When he pulled the two sides apart, Ode fell onto the snow.

"Ode," Nim said. "You're all right."

"But I'm small," Ode called sadly up into the sky. "Even smaller than before."

"That'll wear off in a day or two," the salesman said before clapping his hands over his mouth, as if to stop more of the truth from bubbling out.

Blink scooped Ode up and put him in his pocket.

With the giant released, Blink, Nim, and Otto began to search through the bag for something—or someone—else.

At last, Otto found the orb he sought. "Mother?"

A little woman sat inside the glass, knitting together some cloth. Her long brown hair was tied in a plait. Her red coat was gone, and her dress was all tattered. Even though he hadn't stopped searching for his mother, deep down Otto had feared it was a pointless task. But now he could see it hadn't been. His greatest dream—his biggest wish—had come true. He'd found his mother. And this time, unlike in the summer wood, it was real.

Otto's mother did not respond as her son called out her name. It was like she was trapped in a world of her own. She didn't even notice as the orb was lowered to the ground, and barely stirred as it was tapped on the forest floor three times.

When the orb cracked and Otto pulled the sides apart, his mother dropped onto the ground. She was smaller than his shoe.

Released from the orb that had trapped her for three months, Marta looked up at the world around her. She squealed and jumped away when she saw the three giants. Then she recognized a face.

"Otto? Is that you?"

"Mother!" Otto cried. He wanted to scoop her

up in a hug but was afraid he would squash her. He lowered his hand to the ground, and she stepped onto his palm. She hugged one of his fingers as he lifted her into the air.

"What's happened?" Marta said. Otto's face was as large as the moon. "You've turned into a giant."

"No, I haven't. You've been shrunken down. But don't worry, you'll grow back."

"I can't believe it's really you," his mother said. She reached out with her tiny hands and touched his face. "My little Otto has grown so big. I missed you more than anything."

"I missed you too," Otto said. "I never stopped looking for you."

"And now you've found me." His mother smiled at him. "I'll never leave you again."

Otto placed his mother carefully in his pocket. They were ready to leave, but there was still one problem.

"Please, can I have my bag back?" the traveling salesman said. "I need to go." He looked up at the setting moon and gulped. It would be dawn soon.

"Why should we give it back?" Nim said.

"Because I have to go. If I don't make it to the end of the path before the sun rises, I'll disappear and never come back. It's the curse of being a traveler. I can live forever, if I only appear for one night a month."

Nim didn't mind the sound of the traveling

salesman disappearing forever. After all, it was clear he was not a very nice man. But she also didn't want to be responsible for causing something like that.

"I'll give the bag back," Nim said. "But on one condition."

"Anything," the salesman said. But then honesty got the better of him, and he clarified: "Almost anything."

"You have to let all of your shrunken things go. And you can't steal anything else."

"But that's what I do," the salesman said. "I steal things and shrink them down. That's all I'm good for."

"Then you can't have your bag," Nim replied.

"Fine," the salesman snarled. "I won't have my bag. But please let me go. I don't want to disappear into the dawn."

"All right," Nim said. She turned to the wolves. "You can let him go. Besides, he won't be able to do much without his bag of things, and he doesn't have any orbs."

"Thank you," the salesman said. "Thank you very much." He stood to leave, but Nim had one final question.

"Wait," she said. "You said something before about losing a sundragon."

"Oh yes," he said. For the first time, the traveling salesman actually looked sad.

"What do you mean? What happened to it?"

"Fifty years ago, on a full moon like this, a group of humans entered the woods in search of eight missing men. They stumbled upon me and thought I was the murderer. Before I could trap them in an orb, they trapped me in a cage and started to wheel me back to the city. They stopped for a break and left a young woman to keep watch. I told her she could choose any of my orbs and keep it for free if she let me go. So that's what she did. She unlocked the cage and let me out. She chose the orb with a baby sundragon inside: the last sundragon I ever found. I have no idea what she did with it. But I do know this. Ever since I lost that sundragon, the world has been growing colder. One day it will grow so cold everything will freeze."

Nim thought back to what the wolves had told her. They had said they believed a human was behind the cold. At the time, Nim didn't think any human would have the power to take away the heat of the sun. But maybe a human who had a sundragon could.

"What was the woman's name?" Nim asked as her heart began to beat faster.

"Flora Ferber," he said.

And Nim's heart lurched in response.

✦ Chapter Thirty ✦

THE SECOND CELLAR

"**W**e need to find out what happened to that sundragon," Nim said to Otto and Blink. Night lay heavy around them. The wolves had gone deeper into the woods to sleep, and little Ode was leading them back to the city.

Eager to escape from the forest full of lost things, they walked quickly through the trees. They feared that if they waited too long they would encounter another dangerous creature and might never make it back home.

"Do we really?" Otto asked. Now that he had his mother back, he just wanted things to return to normal.

"Things won't be normal if we don't find out what happened. You heard what the salesman said. The

+ 218 +

world will keep growing colder. Eventually, every day will feel as cold as a coldstorm. We'll all freeze."

"What should we do?" Blink asked.

"I'm not sure," Nim said. "But if Frau Ferber is behind this, we have to go to the factory."

"Maybe we can help the other children while we're there," Otto said. "But how are we going to get inside?"

"Easy," Nim said. "We'll knock on the front door."

"I don't think this is a good idea," Otto whispered to Nim.

The three children stood on the front step of Frau Ferber's factory. All the windows above were black. Everyone was in bed.

"Trust me," Nim whispered back. "I've got a plan."

Before Otto or Blink could talk her out of it, Nim reached out and knocked sharply on the front door. When nothing happened, she knocked louder. Eventually, they heard footsteps approaching the door and saw a flicker of light through one of the windows.

"Run!" Nim said.

The three of them raced down the street and hid behind the corner of the building. They had just darted out of sight when the factory door opened.

Heinz stepped down onto the street. A pool of flickering light surrounded him.

"Hello?" He held out his lantern and looked up and down the road, so focused on seeing a person he failed to note the small rat hiding in the shadows.

Nibbles scrambled up the boy's trouser leg and untied the keys that hung from his belt. When the chain fell loose, Nibbles launched himself onto the ground and scurried off along the cobbles.

"Is anyone there?" Heinz called into the empty street.

When no one answered, he turned around and went back inside. The door closed and then reopened.

A confused-looking Heinz stepped outside. Instead of looking up the road, he looked down at the cobbles, searching for something.

"What the . . . ?" Heinz mumbled. He couldn't see anything on the ground. He raised his hand to his empty belt to check if he had been mistaken. Maybe the keys were still there? When they weren't, he scratched his head.

"What are you doing?" Helmut yelled from inside the factory. His brother was taking so long Helmut had come to check if everything was all right.

"I've lost my keys. I must have had them when I came down. How else could I have unlocked the door?"

Helmut joined Heinz on the front step. He, too, held a lantern. They looked around the factory entrance but could see no sign of any keys.

"You're such a dunce," Helmut said. "Mother's not going to be happy about this."

"You won't tell her, will you?" Heinz asked.

"I won't have to. It won't take long for her to realize you can't open any of the doors. Come on." He turned from the street. "It's too cold and dark. We'll search again in the morning."

The boys went back inside. Helmut locked the door. The light of the lanterns passed by a window upstairs and then went out. The factory grew dark.

Nim, Blink, and Otto left the shadows and ran up to the front, where Nibbles was triumphantly dragging a set of keys.

"That was your best steal yet," Nim said.

"Even I couldn't have done a better job," Blink agreed.

"Hear, hear!" Ode said as his little head peered out from beneath Blink's coat.

"Absolutely splendid," Otto's mother agreed. She was still in her son's coat.

Nibbles handed the keys to Nim before scurrying into her pocket.

Nim glanced up at the factory. Certain no lights were on, she put the longest key in the lock. The front door clicked open.

Nim, Blink, and Otto stepped into the factory. Blink lit his lantern, and the factory floor came into sight.

"It's so warm in here," Blink said. "Almost as warm as the summer wood."

"What do we do now?" Otto whispered.

"We search for the orb," Nim said.

They searched the factory floor first. The only glass they found was the jars used to store the boot polish. They rose to the second floor, which held the sleeping quarters. The children slept in one room. On the other side of the landing were another two rooms. One was Frau Ferber's bedroom; the other belonged to her sons.

"The orb won't be in our old bedroom," Otto said. "Frau Ferber would never keep anything precious in there. If it's in any bedroom, it will be in one of them." He nodded to the two doors at the other end of the landing. None of the children wanted to go in there, but they knew they must. Otto wasn't the greatest at sneaking about and stealing things. But someone else was. "Do you think you can do it, Blink?"

"Of course. I am the best thief, after all. And the quickest."

While Nim unlocked the door to Heinz and Helmut's room, Blink took off his shoes. He handed the lantern to Otto. Its light would surely wake the sleeping brothers up.

"Wish me luck," Blink said as he slipped into the room.

Heinz and Helmut were quiet sleepers. They didn't snore as Blink darted on tiptoes around the room. The full moon's light shone through the window and provided just enough illumination to see. Blink ran his hands along the dresser and searched every drawer. There were only clothes inside. He also peered under the two beds—nothing—and then checked the table between them. All it held was two lanterns, dark but still warm from their recent trip to answer the front door.

"Did you find it?" Nim whispered when Blink stepped back out onto the landing.

Blink shook his head.

Nim locked the first room and then unlocked the second. Blink pushed open the door and slunk inside.

Frau Ferber snored lightly in her bed as Blink searched the space. She owned a lot more things than her sons: three dressers, two large mirrors, an ornate bedside table, and another table near the window. Blink found fancy clothes, expensive jewels, and lots of little trinkets, each worth more than everything he owned. But he failed to find a glass orb.

"She must keep it in her study," Nim said when Blink told her the bad news.

They climbed to the top floor and unlocked the study. With no people sleeping inside, they were able to keep the lantern lit as they searched. Nim pulled open one of the table drawers. She found the ledger inside and also a pot of ink.

"What are you doing?" Blink hissed when Nim opened the book and then the ink.

"Fixing the numbers," Nim said. She'd found the countings for this week and quickly changed some ones to sevens and threes to eights. Hopefully, that would help a few of the children pass.

When Nim was finished, they searched the final drawer of the desk. But all it held was paper and spare ink. They were about to leave when Nim caught sight of something on the mantel.

"I've found it," she said. Nim held up a small glass orb. It was the same size as the ones that had held Ode and Marta. But there was a problem. It was broken. Empty.

"She's already let it out," Otto said. "But where?"

"It can't be in the factory," Blink said. "We've already searched every room, and we know it's not in the cellar. We would have seen it when we hid during the coldstorm."

"But it must be here," Nim said. "The factory is the hottest place in the city. I've never seen a fire, and no smoke rises from the chimneys. Something else is keeping it warm. Something like a sundragon."

"But where is it?" Otto asked. "Surely it would be hard to hide."

"It's true." Ode had been following their

conversation from the safety of Blink's coat. "Sundragons are very large. You couldn't fit them in a room."

"We must be missing something," Nim said. "Let's search again."

They rechecked the rooms they had just searched. They even checked the cellar. But there was no sign of a sundragon. Luckily, they did discover something.

"The factory gets warmer the lower we go," Blink said as they stood on the ground-floor landing. "That's not meant to happen. Hot air rises, not falls."

"So if the sundragon's here, it must be below us," Nim said.

Blink nodded.

"But that doesn't make sense. We're on the lowest floor."

They all began to study the ground. They were hoping to find a trapdoor, but instead, Blink found a piece of black ribbon.

"What's this?"

"That's Bertha's," Otto said. "She's the one who traded places with me. She escaped the factory weeks ago."

"I never saw her," Nim said. "And none of the other tattercoats bumped into a new girl on the streets. They would have noticed her if she got out."

"Why's her ribbon here?" Otto asked. He knelt

down and searched the floor. Bertha had owned two ribbons. Maybe if he found the second one, it would lead them to her.

"I don't think it's here," Otto said when he had searched every section of the floor. He was just sticking his fingers under the molding to see if any ribbon had caught beneath there when the wood moved. "This isn't a wall," Otto said.

The three of them began to push against the wooden panel. They could feel it moving, but it wouldn't open. Eventually, one of them pushed at just the right point. One side of the panel popped out of place and swung open. A staircase appeared, leading down into the darkness.

The three of them looked at one another, as if to see who would go first. Eventually, Nim sighed and took the first step. The others followed. The lower they went, the warmer it became, until they were all sweating. Ode, Marta, and Nibbles had to stick their heads out of the pockets just so they could breathe.

The stairs led to a large metal door. It was bolted and sealed shut with a lock. Nim searched the keys for one that would fit. She slipped a small silver key into the lock. The door clicked open, and a wave of heat washed out.

Nim, Blink, and Otto hesitated. Even though they could sense they were on the right track—they just had to follow the heat—they were nervous. What were they going to find?

Blink raised his lantern. Frau Ferber's second cellar was a lot larger than her first. It stretched beneath the entire factory.

Slowly, they edged inside. With each step they took, the heat grew until it felt like they stood in front of a roaring fire. Then they heard talking up ahead.

Nim, Blink, and Otto were seen before they saw who was watching them.

"Otto?" a voice cried from the darkness. A moment later, a boy appeared in the flickering light. As he ran toward them, his face grew brighter.

"Gunter?" Otto said. He couldn't believe it. It was his lost friend: the one who'd shared his dinner with him after his first day working in the factory. Otto had never thought he would see him again.

Gunter and Otto hugged each other so hard that Otto almost squashed his mother, who was still in his pocket.

"You didn't disappear," Otto said.

"None of us did."

Gunter led them farther into the cellar. Slowly, a group of faces appeared in the dark. Some were children, and some were adults, all of them dressed in the same clothes they had been sent to the cellar in. They looked even tattier than the tattercoats.

"This is where Frau Ferber sends us when our hands get too big," Gunter said. "She sent Bertha down here too." He pointed to a girl standing toward the back of the group. "That's why no one ever came to rescue us. Bertha never had a chance to tell anyone."

At the realization that Bertha had never escaped the factory, Nim felt a wave of guilt wash over her. This guilt grew as she stared at the people before her. When she'd escaped all those years before, she hadn't just left the children upstairs behind. She'd left all the people trapped down here. She wished she had come to rescue them sooner.

Unaware of Nim's thoughts, Gunter continued.

"Frau Ferber said she was going to feed us to Maegen. That's what she calls the creature that lives down here. But Maegen would never eat us. She even shares her food. That's how we've stayed alive."

"Can we meet her?" Nim asked.

Gunter nodded. "She's a little farther in. Come on. We'll show you."

The group of children walked deeper into the cellar. Eventually, the dirt gave way to a wall of scales. The scales were red, orange, and yellow. The shape of legs appeared, then wings, and then a head.

Maegen's head was adorned with the same scales that covered her body. She opened her eyes as they neared. Her pupils churned a fiery yellow, even brighter than the sun. Heat pulsed off her.

The three of them gasped. They had found the last sundragon.

"We think she's sick," Gunter said.

"It's true," a young woman added. Her skin was paler than the moon. "When I was sent down here five years ago, Maegen would move around, and the flames in her eyes would dance. But she's been growing slow and weak. A sundragon wasn't made to live in darkness. None of us were."

"We have to get out of here," Gunter said. "Maegen too."

"But how?" the older girl said. "There's only one door, and Maegen's too big to fit."

Otto and Blink didn't know what to do, but Nim had an idea. She reached into the bag they had taken from the traveling salesman and pulled out an empty orb. Fifty years ago, one of the orbs had trapped the poor sundragon. Now Nim would use another to set her free.

Blink peered out into the hidden stairway.

"All clear," he called over his shoulder.

All the people Frau Ferber had sent to the cellar stepped through the open door. Nim was the last to leave. She shut the cellar door behind her and climbed to the ground floor. When they emerged from the hidden space, the front door was only yards away. In a few seconds, they would be free. But Otto knew they couldn't leave yet.

"We can't leave the others behind. We need to get them out."

Nim agreed. This was their chance to help all the children escape. They couldn't leave a single one behind.

The rotting floorboards creaked as Nim, Otto, and Blink climbed to the second floor. They stepped onto the landing, and Nim used the stolen keys to unlock the door.

Frau Ferber's children were huddled in their beds when the door opened. When they didn't hear Heinz or Helmut yelling, one of them peered toward the doorway.

"Nim?" a quiet voice said. "Is that you?"

Nim peered into the darkness. She could just make out the shape of a small boy in a large coat. Despite the heat of the factory, Skid had not taken it off. He had been trapped in the factory for the same amount of time as they had been trapped in the forest.

"Skid!" Nim said. She wanted to yell the word with joy, but she had to keep quiet so that she wouldn't wake Heinz and Helmut. She searched among the other faces and saw Roe. They were both okay. "Come on," she said. "All of you. Up you get. It's time to go."

Nim waved the children toward the door, but they didn't move. Their eyes were open wide with wonder and fear. Mouse looked the most fearful of all. Things didn't go well for him when he broke the rules.

"We'll get in trouble," Roe said. "Frau Ferber will punish us."

"She won't be causing you any more trouble. Trust me." Nim held up the stolen keys, including the one for the front door.

The children grabbed their measly belongings and quietly scattered from the room. Mouse was the first out the door. He'd already had his tongue stolen; he wanted to get out before Frau Ferber stole anything else. He gave a huge smile of thanks as he hurried into the hallway. The other children filed out onto the landing and realized Nim wasn't alone.

"Gunter?" Frida said when her eyes fell upon her lost friend. "You didn't disappear!"

She gave him a warm hug. When she stepped back, she recognized more of the faces. All the disappeared children were there; not even one had been lost.

Eager to escape the factory, they hurried downstairs. This time when they neared the front door, Nim didn't turn away. She drew the largest key from the chain and slipped it into the heavy brass lock. The door creaked open.

All the children—the children with little hands

and big hands, the children who had worked in the factory for years and the children who had lived in the darkness below for so long they weren't even children anymore—raced out into the night.

High above, the windows of the factory remained dark. Frau Ferber and her sons were sleeping so soundly in their comfy beds they hadn't even heard them leave.

Chapter Thirty-One

THE SUMMER NIGHT

On the night they escaped Frau Ferber's factory for the final time, Nim, Otto, and Blink left the city behind and headed for the woods. They stopped when they reached the first row of trees.

In the time they had spent in the factory, Ode and Marta had grown. Now they each stood a foot tall.

"That's better," Ode said as he was lowered to the ground. He squeezed his toes into the snow.

"Are you sure you don't want to stay with us?" Nim asked. She had grown quite fond of the shrunken giant.

"Better not," Ode said. "I quite like sleeping in my old shoe."

Though Ode was returning to the woods, he wasn't returning alone. Nim pulled a glass orb from her pocket and tapped it three times on the forest floor. The last sundragon fell onto the ground, and the snow melted around her. She let out a tiny plume of smoke in thanks and stretched her little wings.

"Take good care of her," Nim said to Ode as the little giant picked up the sundragon. "You two can grow big together."

"You can also release all of these," Blink said. He handed the salesman's bag to the giant. All the things the traveling salesman had captured would soon be free.

"Gosh, this will keep me busy," Ode said. The kind giant smiled up at his new friends. He was going to miss them. He hoped they'd visit his shoe soon.

The friendly giant waved goodbye and turned around. With every step he took, the snow melted around him and the trees above sprouted leaves. The larger Maegen grew, the warmer the world would become.

As Ode continued deeper into the woods on the way back to his shoe, he passed by a witch's den, and a little piece of summer trickled inside.

Islebill's eyes lit up, and she cackled with delight when the warm breeze blew through her open window.

"I smell summer," she said with a blackened smile.

Despite the late hour, she left her cottage and danced around the clearing. The snow was melting. Soon, she would be strong, and she could lure whoever she wanted back to her home. First on the list would be those two sneaky children who had outwitted her.

Unfortunately for Islebill, she wasn't strong yet. As she cackled and danced by her well, she lost her footing and fell right in. At the exact moment she hit the bottom, seven wolves lost their fur and turned back into men.

With Ode and Maegen now safe, Nim, Blink, Otto, and Marta left the edge of the forest and headed back into the city. Hodeldorf already felt warmer than it had in years. Snow, which had lain like paint atop the rooftops for decades, was beginning to melt. Little streams of water spilled off the gutter and ran down the streets. The never-ending winter was beginning to wash away.

"You can share my chimney tonight," Nim offered as they wandered through the city.

"I think we can do better than that," Marta said from where she hid inside her son's coat. "We can all stay at the inn. The traveling salesman may have traded my coat, but he didn't take my coins."

Before they went to the inn, they made one final stop along the way. Even though it was a dastardly place, Frau Ferber's factory had brought them all together.

"What are we doing here?" Otto asked when they stopped before the grimy factory.

"You'll see," Nim said. Releasing Maegen from

one orb had given her an idea about how to use another.

For the first time in decades, the factory was empty of all the children who had slaved away inside. Only one greedy woman and two greedy sons remained. Soon, they would wake up and realize the children were gone. It wouldn't be long before Frau Ferber was back to her old tricks: taking poor children in to staff her factory. Nim couldn't let that happen.

Nim pulled a glass orb from her coat. Before Blink had handed the bag of orbs to Ode, she'd slipped one of the empty ones into her pocket. She hadn't stolen it. She'd been gifted it, in a way, for providing a service: a service to the shrunken and lost creatures of the woods. She knew exactly what to fill it with.

With more force than she'd ever mustered, Nim threw the orb at the factory. The glass hit the front door, and the entire building—brick walls, glass windows, and quiet chimneys—was instantly sucked inside. With a clatter, the orb fell to the ground.

Nim couldn't whistle like the traveling salesman. Instead, she picked up the orb with her hand, shoved it in her pocket, and hurried off with her friends into the night. Where the factory had once stood was now nothing more than an empty square.

EPILOGUE

One Year Later

Nim skipped along the streets of Hodeldorf. The sun had set, and a summer breeze danced through the city. She'd just come back from visiting a very friendly and very tall giant in the woods. She wasn't scared of the forest anymore. It was there that they had found all the things they had lost. Otto had found his missing mother. Nim had found a new family. And Blink had found a way to be welcomed back into the tattercoats.

Nim turned onto Wintertide Lane. Instead of going to number twenty-seven, she went to number twenty-eight.

"I'm back!" she called as she stepped inside. Nibbles sat proudly on her shoulder. It was so warm tonight, neither of them needed their coats.

"Just in time," Marta said. "Dinner's almost ready."

Nim helped Blink and Otto clear the table. It was covered in cloth and thread. After one year in the city, Marta was now known as the best coat maker in Hodeldorf. The residents didn't need quite as many coats as before, but they did still need coats to keep them warm in winter.

Nim had become quite a deft hand at making coats. Now she was officially Marta's assistant. When she wasn't working for paying customers, she was busy patching the coats that belonged to the tattercoats. Not only that, but Sage had promoted her. Once a week, she got to teach the other tattercoats reading and writing. And at the end of each lesson, she taught them a story. Only her stories weren't fairy tales like Sage's. She told them true stories about all the magical things that had happened to her, Otto, and Blink while they were in the woods. The children liked the story of Islebill the most and laughed every time she turned into a chicken.

Nim helped Marta finish cooking dinner. When it was ready, she carried an extra pot outside.

"Dinner's ready!" she yelled up toward the roof. The tiles clattered like a symphony, and a bunch of little heads appeared over the side.

"Smells delicious!" Roe called.

"Like sausages." Skid licked his lips.

Nim hooked the pot of stew onto a long rope and

hoisted it up to the roof. Above, Sage yelled for the tattercoats to get in line. Two minutes later, the empty pot was lowered.

"Thanks," Sage called down with a wave.

Nim smiled and headed back inside. She failed to note the looks of disapproval coming from the house across the road. The Vidlers were not at all happy with their new neighbors. Every time they looked outside, they saw a motley crew of tatty children waving at them.

"We really must move, Hans," Frau Vidler said as she closed the curtains and tied them shut.

Across the road, Nim took her place at the table. The window was open, and a warm breeze trickled into the room. The fire was unlit. Little trinkets covered the mantel above: some Otto had brought with him from Dortzig and others they had found on the streets of the city. Right in the center, next to a clock, which had been bought instead of stolen, stood a little orb with a black factory inside. If you held it up to the morning light and looked very closely, you could just make out a little old woman and two nasty young men scurrying about in thick coats. With no sundragon to keep the factory warm, it was as cold as a coldstorm in there. The Ferbers were trapped in their own little world, and for Nim, Blink, and Otto, things were at last right within their own.